AS I LOOK INTO YOUR FACE

My Jesus, O' my Jesus, as I look into your face

I see that day is setting on the whole human race

Yet you call into the darkness, to see if there is one

Who will hear your voice and answer

Your call to salvation

Your Bride is making ready, the door is open wide

She is standing right there with you

Close to your side

She is clothed with your glory, radiant as the sun

She extends her hand to all men, imploring them to come

She travels every byway, declaring Jesus name

Calling men from their despair

To leave their sin and shame

Soon the door will be closed

Time will come to and end

The only ones left standing

Will have made you their friend

1

THE STORY OF THE LOST NICKEL

I was told a silly story some time ago. You may have heard it.
A man lost a nickel and was looking for it on the ground.
Another man came along and noticed that the man looking for something.
The second man asked the first man what he was looking for.
The first man said he was looking for a nickel that he had lost.

The second man began to look for the nickel on the ground
In the same vicinity of the first man.
After a time, when the second man could not find the nickel,
He asked the first man where, exactly, he had lost the nickel.
The first man said that he had lost the nickel in another another adjacent place.

The second man then said:
Why are you looking here, if you lost the nickel over there?
The first man said to the second:
Because the light is better over here.

This story, at first glance seems to be absurd.
However, there are times when many of us are caught in such an absurdity.
We are looking for something that cannot be found where we are looking,
But the light seems good.
This is always the tendency of mankind, assisted by the deception of Satan.
He masquerades as an angel of light but his light is darkness and leads to death.

Adam and Eve had everything that was good,
But the Serpent convinced them that there was something more.
The light seemed to be better where the serpent was leading.

The Jews in Jesus' day had the light of Old Testament books,
The law of Moses and their traditions,
Which provided more light to them than the revelation of their Messiah.

Today, God has given this generation a completed Scripture,
And a marvelous New Covenant.
However, this generation will have to be in right relationship with Christ Jesus
To correctly interpret The Season Of The Last Generation.
The condition of the heart of each person will determine
If they are in the right place or where the light may seem better.

All the wiles of Satan are currently being employed to deceive this generation.
His False Church is masquerading as an angel of light.
This is his last and final opportunity to subvert the work of Christ Jesus!
But he fails, the gates of hell will not prevail against the Church of Christ, Hallelujah!

FORWARD

Part of what I write in this book was included in my previous book entitled
"The Time Of The END."
However, the Spirit of the Lord wanted to describe
The Season Of The Last Generation in more depth,
Which is what I have endeavored to do.

Regardless of when the "Season" occurs,
Christians are to live a consistent and Godly life
Allowing Christ to live in an through them.
Nevertheless, Christ Jesus warned Christians to watch for the "Season"
So that they would not be caught off guard.

This "watching" has been made more complicated
Since Christians at many different times during the last 2,000 years
Have thought that they were living in The Time Of The END;
So, many people have announced the coming of The Time Of The END,
And certainly, there have been many dark times in the last 2,000 years.

This is similar to the children's story where the child cries out "wolf", "wolf,"
And people come running to the child's defense only to find no "wolf."
This happens enough times,
That the people stop coming to the child's defense when she cries "wolf;"
Then the wolf really comes and the child cries "wolf,"
And no one comes to her defense and the wolf consumes the child.
Jesus said that such will be the case when the "trap" is sprung;
The Holy Spirit is taken out of the world,
And the Antichrist takes control; it will be unexpected.

Christ Jesus said:
No one knows about that day or hour (when He will come again),
Not even the angels in heaven, nor the Son, but only the Father
Be on guard! Be alert! *You do not know when that time will come.*
It's like a man going away: He leaves his house in charge of his servants,
Each with his assigned task, and tells the one at the door to keep watch.

Therefore keep watch because you do not know
When the owner of the house will come back--
Whether in the evening, or at midnight, or when the rooster crows, or at dawn.
If he comes suddenly, do not let him find you sleeping.
What I say to you, I say to everyone: Watch! *(Mark 13:32-37)*

CONTENTS

The Season Of The Last Generation

"Lord I thank You for Your Word, it is the food and bread of LIFE.
Even as You Lord Jesus are the food and the bread of LIFE.
Bless your Word to our hearts, to our souls, to our minds,
To our spirits, in Jesus name.
Help us, enable us, move us to do your will O' God.
Amen and amen."

*The Scriptures used in this book are from the New International Version and typically italicized. Words in parentheses (and not italicized) are the interpretation of the author. The author also bolds and underlines Scriptures for the emphasis he believes of special importance.

THE OVERVIEW OF THE 'SEASON'

The Season Of The Last Generation

Christ Jesus said that every Christian would be able to know the "Season"
Immediately preceding The Time of The End.
He said that the generation living in this "Season,"
Would be the generation to whom the The Time of The END would come.

Since the ascension of Christ Jesus we have been in the Last Days,
That is, the last two days, the last two thousand years of "Time."
The apostle Peter said that to the Lord, a day is like a thousand years,
And a thousand years like a day.
In creation God worked for six days and rested on the seventh,
Likewise, God the Father has worked with mankind
For 6,000 years of Scriptural history,
And it is time for His millennial rest of a thousand years.
God's rest brings "Time" to an END.

The other prophetic event that is required before The Time of The END
Is the reconstitution of Israel as a nation that occurred in 1948.

Therefore the two prophetic events that set-up The Time of The END are:
- The end of the 6,000 years of Scriptural history, and the last two days, or the last 2,000 years that began at the birth of Christ Jesus.
- The reconstitution of Israel as a nation.

These two events have never been present before this time.
The other natural reality that has never been present before
Is the ability of mankind to destroy themselves with nuclear weapons.

The time table that Christ Jesus gave us from Scripture is as follows:

- The Beginning of Birth Pains.
- The "Season;" the "Lesson from the Fig Tree."
- The Ministry of The Bride of Christ for three and one-half years.
- The "Apostasy / Rebellion" in the Church of God.
- Because of the Apostasy / Rebellion in the church of God the Holy Spirit is removed from the earth.
- This allows Satan to reveal his Antichrist, the Beast.
- Then the Antichrist, the Beast, sets up his "image," the "Abomination That Causes Desolation," in the Church.
- The Bride of Christ is taken into the "desert," for the period of the Tribulation.
- The Great Tribulation commences.
- At the end of The Great Tribulation, Christ Jesus comes again, to The Battle of Armageddon.

The Season Of The Last Generation

- At The Battle of Armageddon, Christ Jesus defeats the Antichrist and his armies; the armies of all the nations of the world; all His enemies.
- Satan is bound for a thousand years.
- The Wedding Banquet of the Lamb and His Bride.
- The Millennial Reign of Christ Jesus.
- The Final Judgment.
- The New Heavens and the new earth.

Today, it is critically important for us to understand
The "Season" that precedes "the Abomination that Causes Desolation,"
So that we are prepared for what follows. The "Season" includes the "Apostasy / Rebellion" that occurs in the Church of God.

Christ Jesus describes the "Season," "The Lesson From The Fig Tree,"
From Matthew:
- Christians will be persecuted and put to death;
- They will be hated by all nations because they belong to Christ;
- Many Christians will turn away from the faith and betray and hate each other (the Apostasy / Rebellion);
- Many false Christs and false prophets will appear and perform signs and miracles to deceive even the elect If that were possible (which it is not).
- Because of the increase of wickedness the love of most will grow cold, but those who stand firm to the end will be saved.

Lessons From The Gospel Of Mark:
- Christians will be handed over to local councils and flogged in Churches.
- Christians will be brought before governors and kings as a witness to them.
- The gospel will be preached to all nations.
- Whenever Christians are arrested and brought to trial, they are not to worry about what to say because the Holy Spirit will speak through them and for them.
- Brother will betray brother to death, and a father his child.
- Children will rebel against their parents and have them put to death.
- All men will hate those who belong to Christ, but those who stand firm will be saved.

Lessons From The Gospel Of Luke:
- Saints will be sent to prison.
- When brought to trial Christ will give His saints words and wisdom that none of their adversaries will be able to contradict.
- Saints will be betrayed by parents, brothers, relatives and friends, but not a hair of their head will perish.
- The saints must be careful, or their hearts will be weighed down with dissipation, drunkenness and anxieties of life, and the day will close on them unexpectedly like a trap. For it will come upon all those who live on the face

of the whole earth.
- We must always be on the watch and pray that we may be able to escape all that is about to happen; to escape The Great Tribulation and stand before the Son of Man.

The "fig tree" is also representative of Israel as a nation.
The nation of Israel, is at this time, "leafed out," from its former barrenness,
Of nearly two thousand years without a country.

Christ Jesus promised that the Holy Spirit will tell us what is yet to come.
(John 16:13)
The end time events will not take the The Bride of Christ, by surprise.

Many Will Come Claiming To Be The Christ
Christ Jesus says that during the "Season" that precedes The Great Tribulation
No one should believe anyone who says
That He can be found anywhere on the earth.
The return of Christ Jesus, His second coming, will be no mystery;
The heavens will be ablaze.
At the end of The Great Tribulation and before The Battle of Armageddon
He will come and the whole world will see Him.
At the trumpet call of God, He will come on the clouds with power and great glory;
Gathering his elect from heaven and earth.

The Gospel Of The Kingdom Preached To The Whole World
Christ Jesus says that the Gospel of the Kingdom of God
Will be preached to the whole world and then the end will come.
This may not entirely be done through the evangelism of the saints,
Because an angel is sent at the beginning of The Great Tribulation
To preach the gospel to every living person.
Every person on earth will have heard the gospel before the end comes.

Because of the Increase of Wickedness
The Love Of Most Will Grow Cold
Apart from devotion to Christ Jesus there are no answers for the world.
Satan is out to steal from, kill and destroy all mankind,
Masquerading as and angel of light;
Pretending to have the answers mankind is looking for.
He is like the demented doctor who cuts the throat of his patient.
He is in control of the whole world, leading it into ever deeper sin and depravity;
Bringing about greater and greater wickedness
That causes the love of most to grow cold.
Finally, his control of the world;
Every nation and every leader of every nation is made manifest.

The Season Of The Last Generation

The Day Will Close Unexpectedly Like A Trap
The saints must be careful,
Or their hearts will be weighed down with dissipation, drunkenness
And anxieties of life, and the day will close on them unexpectedly like a trap.
For it will come upon all those who live on the face of the whole earth.
People will awake one morning and everything will have changed.
Satan's ownership of the world, through his Antichrist will be consummated.
Life on earth will never be the same again.
Just as Christ Jesus will come at an unexpected time,
So the day of Satan, the day his Antichrist takes over,
Will close like a trap, unexpectedly.
At this point every person on the earth will be forced to make a decision for Christ
Or die eternally.

Many False Christs And False Prophets Will Appear
And Perform Signs And Miracles To Deceive Even The Elect-
If That Were Possible (which it is not)
In the "Season" preceding the take over by the Antichrist
Satan will pull out all the stops;
He will deliver all the deception he can muster.
This is his last chance to kill eternally as many as he can.
He will send forth false prophets, performing miracles,
Of such a magnitude as to deceive even the "elect" if that were possible.
However, it is not.
Those with Christ in them and devoted to Him, will withstand the onslaught.

Those Who Stand Firm To The END Will Be Saved
This "Season" will test the faith of all of us.
Just as the saints of every generation have been tested,
So this generation will be tested.
This is simply the final "test."
However, Christ in you is able to see you through.
Greater is He who is in you than he who controls the world.
We can do all things through Christ who strengthens us.
Christ can do exceedingly and abundantly above what we can think or ask,
Through His power at work in us.
We will overcome by the blood of the Lamb and the word of our testimony.

Family Members, Relatives And Friends Will Betray Each Other
Brother will betray brother to death, and a father his child.
Children will rebel against their parents and have them put to death.
Saints will be betrayed by parents, brothers, relatives and friends,

The Season Of The Last Generation

But not a hair of their head will perish as they hold to Christ.

Many Christians Will Turn Away From The Faith And Betray And Hate Each Other
This is the "Apostasy / Rebellion" that Scripture speaks about.
As wickedness increases and the world falls apart,
Socially, politically, and economically, so will the lives of many Christians.
Their expectations of God will be disappointed in a world gone "mad."
There will be no place to "hide" in the natural.
Christians will deny their faith to "get along" with the culture;
With their friends and neighbors.
This social, political, and economic "pressure" is well under way at this time.
This "pressure" has occurred many times in the past;
We can see it in the Scriptures.
Satan's primary objective is to coerce as many as possible to deny their faith,
Sending as many as possible to their eternal death.
Getting Christians to turn away from the faith, and betray and hate each other,
Is his ultimate achievement.

Christians Will Be Persecuted, Put In Prison And Put To Death
This phenomena has occurred throughout history over the last 2,000 years,
And is occurring at this time in some countries.
Before the END it will occur in every nation of the face of the earth.
In fact the END comes when the last of the saints to be killed is killed.

Christians Will Be Handed Over To Local Councils And Flogged In Churches
There will be great consternation within the Church of Christ.
The "Church" will be confronted by the political powers
And forced to conform to their edicts or disband.
This will bring about the "Apostasy / Rebellion" against Christ Jesus
By those within the "Church" who want to "go along" with the political powers.
This brings into the open the False Church.
The False Church then "disciplines" those who remain faithful to Christ
And will not conform to the False Church.
Thus will begin the inquisitions within the False Church.

Christians Will Be Brought Before Governors And Kings As A Witness To Them.
Christians who will not conform to the edicts of the State,
And who are thought to be a threat to the State,
Will be brought before their leaders as a witness to them.
This will be similar to the apostle Paul standing before Felix.

The Season Of The Last Generation

Whenever Christians are arrested and brought to trial,
They are not to worry about what to say
Because the Holy Spirit will speak through them and for them

Christians Will Be Hated By All Nations
Christians will be hated by all nations because all nations belong to the devil
And the only entity standing in the way of their complete domination
Is the Church of Christ Jesus.
As the deception of the devil increases
And the plight of mankind becomes more desperate,
Christians will become the "scapegoat,"
And will be blamed for the social, political and economic woes of the world.
This phenomena is well underway in every nation on earth.

Christians Must Be On The Watch And Pray
That We May Be Able To Escape The Great Tribulation
Christ Jesus told us that we must always be on the watch
And pray that we may be able to escape all that is about to happen;
To escape The Great Tribulation and stand before the Son of Man.

THE CONDITION OF THE CHURCH OF GOD TODAY

Unless the Lord builds the house, its builders labor in vain.
(Psalm 127:1)

The Spirit of God tells me that the Church today,
With its many forms and flavors,
Is no better prepared for the Second Coming of Christ Jesus
Than the Jewish Religious Establishment was in the time of Christ.
The Church that Christ Jesus gave birth to on The Day of Pentecost
Was a "charismatic" Church full of the Holy Spirit and Fire.
This fact was clearly demonstrated throughout the Book of Acts.
The Day of Pentecost was the beginning of a Revival that was to never end.
It has never ended in the hearts of those who belong to Christ;
Those who carry the Fire of His Spirit that He brought.
God has rekindled Pentecost with every Revival He has sent up to this day.
The same Revivals the larger part of the Church has ignored, or persecuted.

In Revival God takes control.
In Revival those who belong to Christ give Him control.
In fact those who belong to Christ fervently pray that He will come and take control.
Any Church can have Revival if they are willing to give Christ control.
Christ Jesus will only take control where He is invited to do so.

The "form" of the Church today is almost universal.
The "form" of the Church today precludes Revival because it demands control.
It has become a platform for the performance of certain men and women.
It is as rigid a "form" as the Church in the time of Christ.

The Jews in Jesus' day had the Old Testament books;
Books in which the Living God poured out His heart to the Jewish people;
Books in which He gave the story of His Christ
Who would come and die for the sins of mankind.
Nevertheless, the religious leaders, the diligent students of the Scriptures,
Could not recognize Christ Jesus when he presented Himself to them.
They worshiped God in vain; it was only rules taught by men.
They were steeped in Law and traditions of Moses.
They were blind to the Scriptures that foretold the coming of the Messiah.
They had determine how the Christ would come and what he would do;
He would come to liberate them from the oppression of the Romans.
In their failure to receive their Messiah they lost everything.

The Season Of The Last Generation

Even those of the religious leaders who believed that Jesus was the Christ,
Would not admit it, because then they would be ostracized from their culture
And loose their high positions in it.
How deceived is that?
They were willing to give up Heaven
For comfort and position in a lost religion and culture, destined for hell.

All of this was made worse,
Because John the Baptist preceded Jesus, announcing His coming.
Many people, and perhaps, especially the tax collectors, prostitutes,
And many of the common people,
Heard the voice of God and went out to John in the wilderness to be baptized.
The religious leaders witnessed all this and remained unmoved.
God sent the Israelites two great revivals, John the Baptist and then Christ Jesus
And the religious leaders ignored them both.

The Church of God was not in good shape even before the last apostle died.
The Seven Letters to the Seven Churches are indicative of that.
The Church was given birth on The Day of Pentecost; enjoyed a period of Glory
And then slide down hill for approximately 1,500 years, until it appeared as dead.
It was then brought to life again by the hand of God
Through a series of Revivals that continue to this day;
God restoring the "Truth" to His Church.
However, the Church is notorious for ignoring
And or persecuting the Revivals that God sends.
The Final Revival will be the three and one-half year ministry of the Bride of Christ
That will precede the Apostasy / Rebellion;
The Abomination that Causes Desolation (the "image" of the Beast)
And The Great Tribulation.

Through the revelation of the "Woman" of Revelation 12, The Bride of Christ,
Christ Jesus reveals Himself in His fullness, in all His Glory.
He will bring forth a new Book of the Acts of the Holy Spirit, in our day,
Through the ministry of His Bride.

The rapture that most of the Church is anticipating
Is not Scriptural and will not happen,
To the complete and terrible dismay of most Christians.
There will be a remnant, the "Woman" of Revelation 12, the Bride of Christ,
Who, after ministering for three and one-half years, will be taken Into the desert;
A place of safety, prepare for Her by God, for the duration of The Great Tribulation,
In accordance with Revelation 12.

The Kingdom of God Is Not A Matter Of Talk But Of Power

The apostle Paul said:
*For the kingdom of God is not a matter of talk but of **power**. (1 Corinthians 4:20)*

This is because Christ Jesus came to destroy the works of the devil
And He does this by His power in His people.
This is clearly seen in the Book of Acts.

Christ Jesus said:
As the Father sent me into the world, I have sent them (His disciples) *into the world. (John 17:18)*

*I have given them the **glory** that you gave me, that they may be one as we are one. (John 17:22)*

*I have given you authority to trample on snakes and scorpions
And to overcome all the power of the enemy; nothing will harm you. (Luke 10:19)*

*I am going to send you what my Father has promised; but stay in the city until you have been clothed with **power** from on high. (Luke 24:49)*

*But you will receive **power** when the Holy Spirit comes on you, and you will be my witnesses in Jerusalem, and in all Judea and Samaria, and to the ends of the earth. (Acts 1:8)*

*When Jesus had called his Twelve together,
He gave them **power** and authority to drive out all demons
And to cure diseases and he sent them out to preach the kingdom of God
And to heal the sick. (Luke 9:1-2)*

**The Church that belongs to God,
Will be a Church with the power of God manifested.**

God Consecrates His Church With His Glory

For the generations to come (including our generation)
This burnt offering (worship) *is to be made regularly
At the entrance to the Tent of Meeting before the Lord.
There I will meet you and speak to you; there also I will meet with the Israelites,
And the place will be consecrated by my glory. (Exodus 29:42-43)*

The Church of God has always been consecrated by His Glory.
If there is no Glory, there is no Church.
The only way anyone knows who the people of God are is the revelation of His Glory.
That is the way it was in the Book of Acts,

The Season Of The Last Generation

That is the way it has been from the Book of Acts on, until today.
Worship in Spirit and in Truth will always bring His Glory.
That is why God seeks those who will worship Him in Spirit and in Truth;
So that He can pour out His Glory on them;
So that unbelievers know where to go to meet God;
So unbelievers will know who belongs to God.

The Joy Of The Lord Is Our Strength

This day is sacred to our Lord.
*Do not grieve, **for the joy of the Lord is your strength**. (Nehemiah 8:10)*

The joy of the Lord comes from the revelation of His Glory.
Without the revelation and manifestation of His Glory we have no strength.
With no strength, we are easy prey for the wiles of the devil.

Where There Is No Revelation The People Perish

Where there is no revelation the people cast off restraint (or perish).
(Proverbs 29:18)

The people of God were never meant to be without revelation,
Manifestation of the Living God.
The people of God were created to live in intimate relationship with their God.
Without this relationship they perish.
In the New Covenant the Holy Spirit was given to those who believe;
He puts His law in their minds and writes them on their hearts,
So that every believer can have intimate relationship with Christ Jesus.
Part of this revelation is personal and part of it is corporate.
The gifts of the Spirit were given to provide corporate revelation to the Body.
Without personal and corporate revelation, manifested, the people perish.

On The Day of Pentecost Peter quoted the Prophet Joel:
In the last days, God says I will pour out my Spirit on all people.
Your sons and daughters will prophesy, your young men will see visions
Your old men will dream dreams.
Even on my servants both men and women
I will pour out my Spirit in those days, and they will prophesy. (Acts 2:17-18)

Christ Jesus is the Spirit of prophesy.
Through His impartation of prophesy, dreams and visions,
He provides "vision" and "revelation" for His Church.
Without this "vision" and "revelation" His people perish.

What Does A New Covenant Assembly Look Like?
The apostle Paul describes it:
When you come together, everyone has a hymn, or a word of instruction,
A revelation, a tongue or an interpretation.
All of these must be done for the strengthening of the church.
If anyone speaks in a tongue, two or at the most three,
Should speak, one at a time, and someone must interpret.
If there is no one to interpret, the speaker should keep quiet in the church
And speak to himself and God.

Two or three prophets should speak,
And the others should weigh carefully what is said.
And if a revelation comes to someone who is sitting down,
The first speaker should stop.
For you can all prophesy in turn
So that everyone may be instructed and encouraged
The spirits of the prophets are subject to the control of the prophets.
For God is not a God of disorder but of peace. (1 Corinthians 14:26-33)

The whole purpose of the people of God assembling
Is to meet with and hear from God,
By His Spirit, through the gifts of the Spirit in His people.
Worship is the catalyst that enables the people of God to get "in the Spirit;"
Then the Spirit of God is able to bring forth His gifts, including
Prophesy, visions, words of knowledge and words of wisdom.
This is how God the Father provides "vision," "revelation,"
And illumination to His Church, without which they perish,
But with which they thrive.

Much of the Church today has reverted to a "form" that precludes
The impartation from Christ Jesus of the continuous revelation
He desires to bring.

The Church In The Day Of Christ Jesus
The Church (Israel) in the day of Christ Jesus was a very religious Church.
They followed the traditions of Moses faithfully,
But they worshiped God in vain because their hearts were far from Him.
They had not had a corporate revelation from God in 400 years.
Their worship consisted of rules made up by men.
They diligently studied the Scriptures
But their study did not enable them to recognize their Messiah.
In fact, they resented Christ Jesus and killed Him;
He got in the way of their religion.

The Season Of The Last Generation

The Church After The Book Of Acts
The Church of God was in trouble before the last apostle died.
This can clearly be seen in the Seven Letters to the Seven Churches
In the Book of Revelation.

The condition of the Church of God, today, in The Season Of The Last Generation,
Is described by Christ Jesus in the Seven Letters to the Seven Churches
In the Book of Revelation.
These seven descriptions, describe the condition of virtually every church today.
Every church today will fall into one category or another or some combination.
Only two of the seven are commended.
Five are given sever warnings.

The condition of many individual Christians today is described in:
- The Parable of the Ten Virgins
- The Parable of the Talents
- The Parable of the Wedding Banquet
- Those Who Will Say Lord, Lord
- The Parable of the Sheep and the Goats
- Many live as enemies of the cross of Christ

To The Church In Ephesus (Revelation 2:1-7)
To the angel of the church in Ephesus write:

These are the words of him who holds the seven stars in his right hand
And walks among the seven golden lampstands:

I know your deeds, your hard work and your perseverance.
I know that you cannot tolerate wicked men,
That you have tested those who claim to be apostles but are not,
And have found them false.
You have persevered and have endured hardships for my name,
And have not grown weary.

Yet I hold this against you:
You have forsaken your first love.
Remember the height from which you have fallen!

Repent and do the things you did at first.
If you do not repent, I will come to you and remove your lampstand from its place.
But you have this in your favor:
You hate the practices of the Nicolaitans, which I also hate.

He who has an ear, let him hear what the Spirit says to the churches.

The Season Of The Last Generation

To him who overcomes, I will give the right to eat from the tree of life,
Which is in the paradise of God.

Christ Jesus tells John to write to the leader of the church in Ephesus;
That it is He who holds the church leaders in His hand,
And walks among the churches.

He tells the Ephesus church leader the things that the church is doing right:
They have worked hard and have persevered;
They cannot tolerate wicked men;
They have tested those who claim to be apostles but are not,
And have found them liars.
They have persevered and have endured hardships for Christ Jesus,
And have not grown weary;
They hate the practices of the Nicolaitans,

However, Christ Jesus holds this against them:
You have forsaken your first love!

He tells them to remember the height from which they have fallen!
Repent and do the things you did from the first,
When they first came to know Him.

The relationship between Christ Jesus and His Church
Is an intimate personal relationship;
It is a love affair, and not a relationship of simply works!
It is like the relationship between an man and a woman when it is as God intended.
It is like the exhilaration that young lovers have when they first fall in love;
Mind, soul and spirit, they are consumed with love for each other;
It is all they can think and talk about.
They long to be with the other person, to be apart is a hardship.
They have intimate and wonderful conversations about everything under the sun.
They trust and rely upon each other;
They are honest and transparent with each other.
Christ Jesus is saying to the church in Ephesus,
This is what you have lost and must regain, if you are to belong to Me.

Then He issues a sever warning:
If they do not repent, He will come and remove their lampstand from its place;
They will be removed from the Kingdom of God, and from before His throne,
Which is where the lampstands of all God's churches reside.
We understand from this that "first love" is of ultimate importance.

Christ Jesus then tells them that they have in their favor
That they hate the practices of the Nicolaitans,

The Season Of The Last Generation

Who think they can live in their worldliness and idolatry
And still belong to Him.

He tells the Church at Ephesus, if you have an ear, hear what I am telling you.
To those who hear, respond and overcome this world and its ways;
Which are dominated by the deception of Satan,
He will give the right to eat from the Tree of LIFE
Which is nourished by the River of LIFE, that contains the Water of LIFE,
That can only be found in the Paradise of God.

Today, we must have ears that hear what the Spirit is saying to us.
Only by our diligence will we maintain the fervency of our first love for Christ;
Only by allowing Christ to live in and through us.
We must hate what Christ hates.
Then we will maintain our lampstand before the throne of God.
Then we will have the right to eat from the Tree of LIFE in the Paradise of God.

To The Church In Smyrna (Revelation 2:8-11)

To the angel of the church in Smyrna write:

These are the words of him who is the First and the Last,
Who died and came to life again.
I know your afflictions an your poverty--
Yet you are rich!
I know the slander of those who say they are Jews and are not,
But are a synagogue of Satan.
Do not be afraid of what you are about to suffer.
I tell you, the devil will put some of you in prison to test you,
And you will suffer persecution for ten days.
Be faithful, even to the point of death,
And I will give you the crown of life.

He who has an ear, let him hear what the Spirit says to the churches.
He who overcomes will not be hurt at all by the second death.

The church in Smyrna is afflicted
By those who claim to belong to Christ but do not.
It is a fact that the True Church is always afflicted by the False Church,
Just as it was in the time of Christ.
The Church in Smyrna is being slandered by the Church of Satan
That pretends to be a Church of Christ Jesus.
They are in poverty, yet are rich in God.
They are going to suffer at the hand of the False Church and be put in prison,
But if they are faithful, even to the point of being killed,
They will receive the crown of LIFE and avoid eternal death.

The Season Of The Last Generation

Today, we also must have ears that hear what the Spirit is saying to us.
We must remember that the only entity
That stands in the way of Satan's complete domination of the world
Is the Church of Christ Jesus.
Because of this, the Church is the focus of Satan's deception,
The rest of the whole world belongs to him.
The synagogue of Satan, the False Church,
Believes that it represents God, but it is deceived, just as it was in the time of Christ.
It believes it can embrace God and the world at the same time, which it cannot.
The Church of Christ Jesus today faces the same trial,
There is nothing new under the sun.
The human condition, in the natural, is one boring repetition after another,
Of mankind rejecting God and His Christ, under the deception of Satan.
The result is hell for all, but those who receive Christ Jesus and live for Him.

To The Church In Pergamum (Revelation 2:12-17)
To the angel of the church in Pergamum write:

These are the words of him who has the sharp, double-edged sword.
I know where you live—where Satan has his throne.
Yet you remain true to my name,
You did not renounce your faith in me,
Even in the days of Antipas, my faithful witness,
Who was put to death in your city—where Satan lives.

Nevertheless, I have a few things against you:
You have people there who hold to the teaching of Balaam,
Who taught Balak to entice the Israelites to sin by eating food sacrificed to idols
And by committing sexual immorality .
Likewise you also have those who hold to the teaching of the Nicolaitans.
Repent therefore!
Otherwise, I will soon come to you and will fight against them
With the sword of my mouth.

He who has an ear, let him hear what the Spirit says to the churches.
To him who overcomes, I will give some of the hidden manna.
I will also give him a white stone with a new name written on it,
Known only to him who receives it.

The sharp double-edged sword is the Word of God, who is Christ Jesus
The impeccable judge of all things.
The Church of Pergamum is in the city where Satan resides and has his throne.
In spite of this, the Church of Pergamum has remained true to Christ Jesus,
Even though their leader was put to death by Satan's emissaries,
The False Church.

The Season Of The Last Generation

However, within the Pergamum Church, there are those deceived,
Who hold to the teaching of Balaam
And are involved in idol worship and sexual immorality.
Some also, are involved with the teaching of the Nicolaitans
And their idol worship and worldliness.
Christ Jesus warns them that unless they repent,
He will come and fight against them,
Revealing them for what they are.
Christ Jesus calls for those of us who have an ear,
To hear what He is saying to the churches.
Those who overcome the deception of Satan,
Will receive some of the hidden manna, the Bread of LIFE.
They will also receive a white stone with a new name written on it,
Known only to him who receives it.
The white stone represents the holiness that Christ Jesus imparts to His own;
The new name is symbolic of the intimate and personal relationship
Between each saint and Christ Jesus.
Each of us will have a name (a nick name given us by Christ),
That is only known by Christ and ourselves.

Today, there are those who believe they can follow Christ Jesus
And do as they please
From the very beginning of the Church
There have been those claim they can live as they please
And remain in the favor of God.
This, is of course, a lie from the deception of the devil.

To The Church In Thyatira (Revelation 2:18-29)
To the angel of the church in Thyatira write:

These are the words of the Son of God, whose eyes are like blazing fire
And whose feet are like burnished bronze.
I know your deeds, your love and faith, your service and perseverance,
And that you are now doing more than you did at first.

Nevertheless, I have this against you:
You tolerate that woman, Jezebel, who calls herself a prophetess.
By her teaching she misleads my servants into sexual immorality
And the eating of food sacrificed to idols.

I have given her time to repent of her immorality, but she is unwilling.
So I will cast her on a bed of suffering,
And I will make those who commit adultery with her suffer intensely,
Unless they repent of her ways.

The Season Of The Last Generation

THE CONDITION OF THE CHURCH TODAY

I will strike her children dead.
Then all the churches will know that I am he who searches hearts and minds,
And I will repay each of you according to your deeds.

Now I say to the rest of you in Thyatira,
To you who do not hold to her teaching
And have not learned Satan's so called deep secrets
(I will not impose any other burden on you):
Only hold on to what you have until I come.

To him who overcomes and does my will to the end,
I will give authority over the nations--

He will rule them with an iron scepter;
He will dash them to pieces like pottery--

Just as I have received authority from my Father.
I will also give him the morning star.
He who has an ear, let him hear what the Spirit says to the churches.

Christ Jesus says to the leader of the Church of Thyatira,
That His words are the words of the Son of God,
Whose all seeing eyes blaze with His holiness;
Who's feet are like burnished bronze,
Speaking of His absolute power and authority.

Christ Jesus tells them He knows everything they have done and continue to do,
That they are now doing more that ever before.

However, in their midst of the Church is a woman, Jezebel
(A Satan deceived, rebellious woman),
Who the Church has allowed a place of authority;
Who claims and pretends to be a prophetess;
Who is misleading His servants into sexual immorality and idol worship.
Christ Jesus has given her a time to repent, but she refuses.
She is about to be afflicted with great suffering,
Along with all those who have committed adultery with her.
Christ Jesus will strike her children dead
(Which could be literal offspring
And/or those who have fallen into sexual sin with her
And/or those who have followed her teaching.)
To let all the churches know that He searches hearts and minds
And repays each person according to what they have done.

The Season Of The Last Generation

Christ Jesus says to those who have not been seduced by Jezebel
And who have not involved themselves with her teaching
And Satan's so called deep secrets
(Satan always pretends to have something more than God),
He will not impose any other burden on them.
He tells them to hold on to what they have (the WAY, the TRUTH and the LIFE),
Until He comes for them.
Those who overcome the deception of Satan and do the will of Christ,
Will be given the authority of Christ over the nations,
They will rule them with an iron scepter (the absolute power and authority of Christ),
They will dash them to pieces like pottery
(The nations will be rendered absolutely powerless and submissive
Because of presence of Christ in the people of God).

Christ Jesus says that just as He received authority from His Father,
He is going to give that same authority to His people.
He is also going to give the Morning Star, which is Himself, Christ in us.
All of us who have an ear, let us hear what the Spirit (Christ)
Says to each one of us and to every Church that claims His name.

Today, like the Church in Thyatira, we must persevere.
We must not be mislead by false prophets within the Church.
We must avoid even the appearance of what is not acceptable to God.
We also, will be rewarded for what we have done whether good or bad.
We can overcome by the power of Christ in us
And rule and reign with Christ when He comes.

To The Church In Sardis (Revelation 3:1-6)
To the angel of the church in Sardis write:

These are the words of him who holds the seven spirits of God and the seven stars.
I know your deeds;
You have a reputation of being alive, but you are dead.
Wake up! Strengthen what remains and is about to die,
For I have not found your deeds complete in the sight of my God.
Remember, therefore, what you have received and heard;
Obey it, and repent.
But if you do not wake up,
I will come like a thief, and you will not know at what time I will come to you.

Yet you have a few people in Sardis who have not soiled their clothes.
They will walk with me, dressed in white, for they are worthy.
He who overcomes will, like them, be dressed in white.
I will never erase his name from the book of life,
But will acknowledge his name before my Father and his angels.

The Season Of The Last Generation

He who has an ear, let him hear what the Spirit says to the churches.

Christ Jesus embodies the seven fold Spirit of God,
He holds the angels, the leaders of His Church, in His hands.
He knows the deeds of the Church in Sardis, which is thought to be alive
By those who look through the eyes of man;
But in reality, in the eyes of God, they are dead.

Christ Jesus tells them to wake up,
And strengthen what remains and is about to die.
He does not find their deeds complete in the eyes of God.
He tells them to remember what they have received and heard;
To repent, of their current situation
And obey what they have received and heard.
If they do not, He warns them that He will come like a thief;
They will not know when He will come.

The few saints in Sardis who have not soiled their clothes
By disobeying what they have received and heard,
Will walk with Christ, dressed in white (His righteousness) for they are worthy.
All those who overcome the deception of Satan,
Will be like them, dressed in white;
Their names will never be erased from the Book of LIFE,
And Christ Jesus will acknowledge their names before His Father and His angels.
All of us who have an ear, let us hear what the Spirit (Christ) says to the churches.

Today, each one of us must be alive in and to God;
We must have zeal and fervency toward God;
The Scriptures teach that Christ's zeal for God consumed Him;
That the Kingdom of God is apprehended by forceful men and women,
Who have set their hearts and minds to please Christ Jesus.
We must obey what we have received and heard.
If we do not, we will be surprised by the coming of Christ.
If we are not prepared to meet Him, there will be terrible consequences.
Yet, all we have to do, is to continue to drink of His Living Water,
Continue to put our faith, hope and trust in Him.
To love Him with all our heart, soul, mind and strength.
Then He belongs to us and we belong to Him
And we can live in the peace of God that passes all human understanding.

The Season Of The Last Generation

To The Church In Philadelphia (Revelation 3:7-13)
To the angel of the church in Philadelphia write:

These are the words of him who is holy and true,
Who holds the key of David.
What he opens, no one can shut;
And what he shuts, no one can open.

I know your deeds.
See, I have placed before you an open door that no one can shut.
I know that you have little strength,
Yet you have kept my word and have not denied my name.
I will make those who are of the synagogue of Satan,
Who claim to be Jews though they are not, but liars--
I will make them come and fall down at your feet
And acknowledge that I have loved you.
Since you have kept my command to endure patiently,
I will also keep you from the hour of trial
That is going to come upon the whole world
To test those who live on the earth.
I am coming soon.
Hold on to what you have, so that no one will take your crown.
He who overcomes I will make a pillar in the temple of my God.
Never again will he leave it.
I will write on him the name of my God
And the name of the city of my God, the new Jerusalem,
Which is coming down out of heaven from my God;
And I will also write on him my new name.

He who has an ear, let him hear what the Spirit says to the churches.

Christ Jesus is holy and true and holds the key of David
(The key to the throne of David, the key to Heaven).
He has the absolute authority over what is shut and what is open.
When He shuts something, it is shut and no one can open it,
And when He opens something, it is open, and no one can shut it.
He holds the keys to death, hell and the grave,
By His perfect knowledge, He determines who goes to Heaven and who goes to hell.

He knows the deeds of the Church at Philadelphia and of every Church today.
For the Church at Philadelphia, He has placed before them, an open door
That no one can shut, even though they have little strength,
Because they have kept His Word and have not denied His name.
Christ Jesus is going to make those who are of the synagogue of Satan,
Who claim to be Jews (Christians) though they are not, but liars;

The Season Of The Last Generation

He is going to make the liars fall down at the feet of the saints
And acknowledge that He loved them.

Because the saints have kept His command to endure patiently,
Christ Jesus is going to keep them from the hour of trial
That is going to come upon the whole world to test those who live on the earth.

[All of a sudden Christ Jesus has jumped to the end of "Time,"
And is talking about The Great Tribulation;
The hour of TRIAL that is going to TEST the whole earth.
This is a promise that those who are true to Him
Will not go through The Great Tribulation.]

Christ Jesus says again, He is coming soon.
He warns His saints to hold on to what they have,
So that no one will take their crown.
If we follow Christ according to His Word, no one can take our crown.
However, we can give away our crown if we give in to the deception of Satan.

Christ Jesus promises that those who overcome,
He will make a pillar in the temple of His God,
Never to leave it for all eternity.
He will write on each saint the name of His God
And the name of the City of His God, the New Jerusalem,
Which will come out of Heaven from God.
Each saint will also have the new name of Christ Jesus written upon him.
Those of us who have an ear, let us hear what the Spirit is saying to His Church.

Today, Christ Jesus offers each one of us an open door that no one can shut.
We too must resist the False Church,
Those who claim to belong to Christ but do not.
We are near to the end of "Time,"
And many of us will be alive when the TRIAL comes upon the earth.
If we are faithful to Christ Jesus we can rest in His peace, without fear.
We can be a pillar in the temple of God
And have His new name written upon us.

To The Church In Laodicea (Revelation 3:14-22)
To the angel of the church of Laodicea write:

These are the words of the Amen, the faithful and true witness,
The ruler of God's creation.
I know your deeds, that you are neither cold nor hot.
I wish you were either one or the other!
So, because you are lukewarm—neither hot nor cold--

THE CONDITION OF THE CHURCH TODAY

I am about to spit you out of my mouth.

You say, 'I am rich, I have acquired wealth and do not need a thing.'
But you do not realize that you are wretched, pitiful, poor, blind and naked.
I counsel you to buy from me gold refined in the fire, so you can become rich;
And white clothes to wear, so you can cover your shameful nakedness;
And slave to put on your eyes, so you can see.

Those whom I love I rebuke and discipline.
So be earnest, and repent.
Here I am! I stand at the door and knock.
If anyone hears my voice and opens the door,
I will come in and eat with him, and he with me.

To him who overcomes,
I will give the right to sit with me on my throne,
Just as I overcame and sat down with my Father on his throne.
He who has an ear, let him hear what the Spirit says to the churches.

Christ Jesus declares that He is the Amen (It will be as I say!),
The faithful and true witness during His time on earth,
And through His people, upon His resurrection,
The ruler of God's creation as the King of kings and Lord of lords.
He knows that the Church of Laodicea is neither hot or cold toward Him,
And wishes that they were either one or the other,
As they would be easier to deal with that way.
Because they are lukewarm, Christ Jesus is about to spit them out of His mouth,
And sever relationship with them altogether;
The cold of course are already lost.

The Laodicean church says of themselves that they are rich and in need of nothing.
However, Christ Jesus finds them wretched, pitiful, poor, blind and naked.
God's view is diametrically the opposite of the Church's view of themselves.
Christ Jesus counsels the Church to come to Him and buy gold refined in the fire;
Allowing the Holy Spirit to put His laws in their minds
And write them upon their hearts.
Then they would become rich in Christ by the power of His Holy Spirit;
They would have gold refined in the fire of His Holy Spirit;
Then the would have white clothes to wear, to cover their shameful nakedness;
Then they would have salve to put on their eyes, so that they could see.
They would have actions and deeds motivated by the Holy Spirit.

Christ Jesus declares that He rebukes and disciplines those He loves;
He always warns them when they have gone astray.
He admonishes them to be earnest and repent;

27

The Season Of The Last Generation

Their very lives are at stake, eternally.
Christ Jesus stands at the door of every person who claims His name and knocks.
Those who hear, open the door to Him, and He comes in and eats with them,
And has intimate communion with them.

To those who overcome this world and its ways
He will give the right to sit with Him on His throne,
Just as He sits at the right hand of God the Father on His throne.
Those of us who have an ear, let us hear what the Spirit is saying to His Church.

Today, unlike the Church of Laodicea, we must be hot for God,
Full of the fire and passion of His Holy Spirit;
An all consuming zeal for God;
Possessing gold refined in the fire of God;
Having actions and deeds that we can present to Christ Jesus,
That have been accomplished through Christ in us.

The Parable Of The Ten Virgins (Matthew 25:1-13)

At that time the kingdom of heaven will be like ten virgins
Who took their lamps and went out to meet the bridegroom.
Five of them were foolish and five were wise.
The foolish ones took their lamps but did not take any oil with them.
The wise, however, took oil in jars along with their lamps.
The bridegroom was a long time in coming,
And they all became drowsy and fell asleep.
At midnight the cry rang out: 'Here's the bridegroom! Come out to meet him!'
Then all the virgins woke up and trimmed their lamps.
The foolish ones said to the wise, 'Give us some of your oil;
Our lamps are going out.'

'No,' they replied, 'there may not be enough for both us and you.
Instead, go to those who sell oil and buy some for yourselves.'

But while they were on their way to buy oil, the bridegroom arrived.
The virgins who were ready went in with him to the wedding banquet.
And the door was shut.

Later the others also came . 'Sir! Sir!' they said. 'Open the door for us!'

But he replied, 'I tell you the truth, I don't know you.'

Therefore keep watch, because you do not know the day or the hour.

This is a parable of The Time of the END; about "virgins," "oil" and "knowing."
The ten were all virgins; that is people washed in the blood of the Lamb; forgiven.

28

The Season Of The Last Generation

Which is the only way that any of us can become virgins in the eyes of God.
The virgins all had some oil in their lamps,
But the only the wise had enough in jars,
To sustain them for the extended period of time that would be required.
They all became drowsy and fell asleep.
At the announcement of the coming of the Bridegroom (Christ Jesus)
They all lit their lamps.

At that time, the foolish virgins realized that they did not have enough oil.
They were not prepared for the occasion.
They ask the wise virgins for some of their oil.
However, the wise refused
Because they said that they may not have enough for all of them.
The wise virgins tell the foolish ones to go and buy oil for themselves.

The foolish virgins go to buy oil.
In the meantime the Bridegroom arrives and there can be no delay;
The five virgins who were ready went in with Him and the door was shut.

Later the five foolish virgins came to the door
And implored the Bridegroom to let them in.
But He replied, that He did not "know" them.

He did not "know" them because they had not allowed
Christ Jesus to write upon their hearts and upon their minds,
Because then, they would have "known" Him and been "known" by Him;
He would have been their teacher according to Jeremiah 31:31-34.
This "knowing" comes by Christ in us our teacher;
Putting His law in our minds and writing it upon our hearts;
It is the anointing, of The Anointed One that teaches us to "know" Him;
It is the oil, a type of the Holy Spirit; Christ in us the hope of glory.
Christ Jesus said,

Now this is eternal life:
That they may _know_ you, the only true God,
And Jesus Christ, whom you have sent. (John 17:3)

The apostle Paul says to the Galatians:
But now that you know God—or rather are known by God-- (Galatians 4:9)

The oil to the five virgins in this case was as critical
As "first love" was to the church of Ephesus.
It is a matter of spiritual LIFE or death before the Christ of God.

The Parable Of The Talents (Matthew 25:14-30)
This parable concerns the status of three servants of Christ Jesus
At The Time of the END.

Again, it will be like a man going on a journey,
Who called his servants and entrusted his property to them.
To one he gave five talents of money,
To another two talents, and to another one talent,
Each according to his ability.
Then he went on his journey.
The man who had received the five talents
Went at once and put his money to work and gained five more.
So also, the one with the two talents gained two more.
But the man who had received the one talent went off,
Dug a hole in the ground and hid his master's money.

After a long time the master of those servants returned
And settled accounts with them.
The man who had received the five talents brought the other five.
'Master,' he said, 'you entrusted me with five talents.
See, I have gained five more.'

His master replied, 'Well done, good and faithful servant!
You have been faithful with a few things;
I will put you in charge of many things.
Come and share your master's happiness!'

The man with the two talents also came.
'Master,' he said, 'you entrusted me with two talents;
See, I have gained two more.'
His master replied, 'Well done, good and faithful servant!
You have been faithful with a few things;
I will put you in charge of many things.
Come and share your master's happiness!'

Then the man who had received the one talent came.
'Master,' he said, 'I knew that you are a hard man,
Harvesting where you have not sown
And gathering where you have not scattered seed.
So I hid your talent in the ground.
See, here is what belongs to you.'

His master replied, 'You wicked, lazy servant!
So you knew that I harvest where I have not sown
And gather where I have not scattered seed?

Well then, you should have put my money on deposit with the bankers,
So that when I returned I would have received it back with interest.

Take the talent from him and give it to the one who has the ten talents.
For everyone who has will be given more, and he will have an abundance.
Whoever does not have, even what he has will be taken from him.
And throw that worthless servant outside, into the darkness,
Where there will be weeping and gnashing of teeth.'

Christ Jesus on The Day of Pentecost poured out His Holy Spirit
On those who believed in Him,
And He has been doing that same thing from that time on;
Giving gifts to men:

Now to each one the manifestation of the Spirit is given for the common good.
To one there is given through the Spirit the message of wisdom,
To another the message of knowledge by means of the same Spirit,
To another faith by the same Spirit,
To another gifts of healing by that one Spirit,
To another miraculous powers,
To another prophecy,
To another the ability to distinguish between spirits,
To another the ability to speak in different kinds of tongues,
And to still another the interpretation of tongues.
All these are the work of one and the same Spirit,
And he gives them to each one, just as he determines. (1 Corinthians 12:4-11)

It is the intent of Christ Jesus
That each of His servants would receive his gift(s) (talent)
And use that gift(s) (talent) to bear fruit for the Kingdom of God.
Those who use their gift(s) (talent) as Christ intended are commended.
Those who do not use their gift(s) are condemned.
Christ Jesus said:
You did not choose me, but I chose you to go and bear fruit--
Fruit that will last. (John 15:16)

I am the true vine and my Father is the gardener.
He cuts off every branch in me that bears no fruit,
While every branch that does bear fruit he trims clean
So that it will be even more fruitful. (John 15:1-2)

The Parable Of The Wedding Banquet (Matthew 22:1-14)
Jesus spoke to them again in parables, saying:
'The kingdom of heaven is like a king
Who prepared a wedding banquet for his son.

31

The Season Of The Last Generation

He sent his servants to those who had been invited to the banquet
To tell them to come, but they refused to come.

Then he sent some more servants and said,
'Tell those who have been invited that I have prepared my dinner:
My oxen and fattened cattle have been butchered, and everything is ready.
Come to the wedding banquet.'

But they paid no attention and went off—one to his field, another to his business.
The rest seized his servants, mistreated them and killed them.
The king was enraged.
He sent his army and destroyed those murderers and burned their city.

Then he said to his servants,
'The wedding banquet is ready but those I invited did not deserve to come.
Go to the street corners and invite to the banquet <u>anyone</u> *you find.'*
So the servants went out into the streets
And gathered all the people they could find, both good and bad,
And the wedding hall was filled with quests.
But when the king came into see the guests,
He noticed a man there who was not wearing wedding clothes.
'Friend,' he asked, 'how did you get in here without wedding clothes?'
The man was speechless.

Then the king told the attendants,
'Tie him hand and foot, and throw him outside, into the darkness,
Where there will be weeping and gnashing of teeth.

For many are invited, but few are chosen.'

God the Father has been inviting people to the wedding of His Son
From the beginning of time.
In the Old Testament, the people doing the inviting were the prophets of old.
The people invited were the people of God, but most of them refused to come.
The people of God mistreated and killed many of the prophets
That God sent to invite them.

John the Baptist came inviting the people of God to the wedding banquet,
And many came to him in the desert confessing their sins
Being baptized; cleansing themselves.
The ones who refused the invitation were the religious leaders of Israel.
John the Baptist was killed for standing for God.

Christ Jesus came inviting the people of God to His wedding banquet.

The Season Of The Last Generation

A few of the people of God received the invitation and received Christ.
However, the religious leaders did not receive their invitation;
They were jealous of Christ Jesus and were responsible for His death.

Because of their treatment of the Son of God;
Because they did not respond to the day of their visitation, their invitation;
In 70 AD their religious rites were taken from them, their temple destroyed,
And they were dispersed to the nations until 1948.

Because the people of God refused the invitation to the wedding banquet
God sent evangelists to the Gentiles;
He sent them to the street corners, to people good and bad.
Because His wedding banquet hall will be filled.

Today, the Father continues to invite the people of God
And whosoever will come, to the wedding banquet.
However, there will be those to busy to come,
Too involved with the things of this world.
There will be those who resent those who invite them to come
And they will mistreat and kill them.

Nevertheless, the wedding banquet will take place,
And everyone who has a heart for God and His Son will be there.
They will have purchased wedding clothes.
They will be clothed in the righteousness of Christ.
No one will be allowed into the wedding banquet without wedding clothes.
In The Time Of The END, just as in all preceding times,
Many will have been called, but few will be chosen.

Not Everyone Who Says Lord, Lord
Will Enter The Kingdom Of God (Matthew 7:21-23)

Not everyone who says to me, 'Lord, Lord' will enter the kingdom of heaven,
But only he who does the will of my Father who is in heaven.
Many will say to me on that day,
'Lord, Lord, did we not prophesy in your name,
And in your name drive out demons and perform many miracles?'
Then I will tell them plainly, 'I never knew you.
Away from me you evil doers!'

Christ Jesus says that MANY will say to Him on that day,
'Lord, Lord, did we not prophesy in your name,
And in your name drive out demons and perform many miracles?'
Yet, the Christ of God will tell them that He never KNEW them,
And calls them EVIL DOERS.

This is one of the most shocking Scriptures in the Bible.
First of all there are not a few, but <u>many</u> in this condition.
These people are exercising gifts that can only be given by the Spirit of God.
They are prophesying, driving out demons, and performing miracles;
They are doing those things that the Scriptures admonish the saints to do.
Yet Christ Jesus does not KNOW them,
And calls them evil doers.

This Scripture teaches us that we can be saved,
Baptized (immersed) in the Spirit;
Christ can put His laws in our minds and write them on our hearts,
Which enables us to KNOW Him;
Yet we can FAIL to do His will.

This FAILURE has everything to do with motive.
If our motive in doing what Scripture calls us to do
Is not done solely out of love for and to please the Christ of God,
Then we are not doing the will of God, no matter what it is.
Doing the will of God is ultimately important.

Scripture teaches that the GIFTS and CALL of God are without repentance.
In other words God gives GIFTS and CALLINGS to men and women as He sees fit.
However, how they use these GIFTS and CALLINGS is in the hands of the person.
If these GIFTS and CALLINGS are not carried out
In LOVE for God and His people, then they are EVIL.

MOTIVE is everything.
If they are done to exalt the person or for monetary gain they are EVIL.

The GIFTS and CALLINGS of God must be done to exalt Christ alone;
They are from Christ, and must exalt Him only.
When they are done to exalt a person this is a LIE
And therefore, perverse and EVIL.

When the GIFTS and CALLINGS of God are used to exalt a person,
That person is following in the foot steps of Satan,
A created being who desires to be exalted and worshiped;
This is a LIE.
Everything he has was given to him by God,
Therefore, for him to take credit for attributes he was given by God,
Is a LIE, EVIL, and condemns that person to eternal death.

The Sheep And The Goats (Matthew 25:31-46)
Jesus said:
When the Son of Man comes in his glory, and all the angels with him,

The Season Of The Last Generation

He will sit on his throne in heavenly glory.
All the nations will be gathered before him,
And he will separate the people one from another
As a shepherd separates the sheep from the goats.
He will put the sheep on his right and the goats on his left.

Then the King will say to those on his right,
'Come you who are blessed by my Father;
Take your inheritance,
The kingdom prepared for you since the creation of the world.
For I was hungry and you gave me something to eat,
I was a stranger and you invited me in,
I needed clothes and you clothed me,
I was sick and you looked after me,
I was in prison and you came to visit me.'

Then the righteous will answer him,
'Lord, when did we see you hungry and feed you,
Or thirsty and give you something to drink?
When did we see you a stranger and invite you in,
Or needing clothes and clothe you?
When did we see you sick or in prison and go to visit you?'

The King will reply, 'I tell you the truth,
Whatever you did for one of the least of these my brothers of mine,
You did for me.'

Then he will say to those on his left,
'Depart from me, you who are cursed, into the eternal fire
Prepared for the devil and his angels.
For I was hungry and you gave me nothing to eat,
I was thirsty and you gave me nothing to drink,
I was a stranger and you did not invite me in,
I needed clothes and you did not clothe me,
I was sick and in prison and you did not look after me.'

They also will answer,
'Lord, when did we see you hungry or thirsty or a stranger
Or needing clothes or sick or in prison, and did not help you?'

He will reply, 'I tell you the truth,
Whatever you did not do for one of the least of these,
You did not do for me.'

Then they will go away to eternal punishment, but the righteous to eternal life.

The Season Of The Last Generation

This parable teaches the sobering reality
Of the love, righteousness and justice of God, the King.
It demonstrates that Christ Jesus completely identifies
With each of His created children, whether they know Him or not,
And all of their needs are of paramount importance to Him.

To supply the needs of others is to supply for Christ Jesus;
To ignore the needs of others is to ignore Christ Jesus Himself.

To be as selfless as Christ Jesus calls us to be, requires that we have His heart;
That we have Christ living inside of us;
That we have been crucified with Christ and no longer live,
But Christ lives in us;
That we do not belong to this world but to His Kingdom,
And we love His children as much as He does.

Christ Jesus is telling us that our eternal destination
Rests on the condition of our heart;
We must have His heart, nothing less will do.

Many Live As Enemies Of The Cross Of Christ

The apostle Paul said:
Join with others in following my example, brothers,
And take note of those who live according to the pattern we gave you.
For, as I have often told you before and now say again even with tears,
Many live as enemies of the cross of Christ.
Their destiny is destruction, their god is their stomach,
And their glory is in their shame.
Their mind is on earthly things.
But our citizenship is in heaven. (Philippians 3:17-20)

Jesus said:
...Anyone who does not take up his cross and follow me is not worthy of me.
Whoever finds his life will lose it, and whoever loses his life for my sake will find it.
(Matthew 10:38-39)

The enemies of the cross that Paul speaks of
Are those who refuse to be crucified to this world
And are therefore of this world, and do not belong to Christ.
This is the same cross that Christ Jesus speaks of.
We each have a cross to bear.
The cross we all must bear is the cross of Christ Jesus;
He was crucified in the flesh by this world,
And we must be crucified in our hearts and spirits to this world.

CHRIST JESUS TELLS HIS PEOPLE TO COME OUT OF BABYLON

Come out of her, my people, so that you will not share in her sins,
So that you will not receive any of her plagues;
For her sins are piled up to heaven, and God has remembered her crimes.
(Revelation 18:4-5)

Depart, depart, go out from there!
Touch no unclean thing!
Come out from it and be pure, you who carry the vessels of the Lord.
(Isaiah 52:11)

If you belonged to the world, it would love you as its own.
But I have chosen you out of the world.
That is why the world hates you. (John 17:16)

The apostle Paul warns the saints:
With many other words he warned them; and pleaded with them,
'Save yourselves from this corrupt generation.' (Acts 2:40)

Have nothing to do with the fruitless deeds of darkness, but rather expose them.
(Ephesians 5:11)

Christians who live for Christ Jesus
Expose the fruitless deeds of darkness of the world
And are therefore hated by the world.

Christ Jesus said:
The world cannot hate you (His natural brothers),
But it hates me because I testify that what it does is evil. (John 7:7)

This is the bottom line.
The world hates Christians because Christians declare to the world
That what they do is evil, and the world cannot tolerate this.
The world will tolerate any sin under the sun,
But they will not tolerate anyone who will not tolerate their sin.
In The Season of the Last Generation this hatred comes to its conclusion.

How To Come Out Of Babylon Today
"Babylon" of the Book of Revelation represents a city and a "system."
The "system" is everything done by mankind under the deception of Satan.
The social, political, and economic systems of the world comprise this "system."
Daniel lived in ancient Babylon, the prototype of all subsequent Babylons.

The Season Of The Last Generation

CHRIST TELLS HIS PEOPLE TO COME OUT OF BABYLON

He was able to live in Babylon and not be of the "spirit" of Babylon which is Satan.
In the case of Daniel, his not being of Babylon was put to the test;
Was he going to continue to pray to his God
Or conform to the edict of the king of Babylon, under the control of Satan,
And stop praying to his God.
Daniel chose to continue praying to his God
And was thrown into the lions den as a result.
However, God saved him out of the lions den because of his faithfulness to God.

This is the situation of most of us.
We live in a world under the control of Satan.
We can continue in to live in the world and have the favor of God,
As long as we do not become of the "spirit" of the world.
This is often difficult,
Because those around us will often put our "faith" to the test.
They will require that we do something unethical, or immoral
And therefore against our God.
This is where the line is drawn; this is where we can give no ground.
We must then refuse to sin against our God,
And trust God to take care of us in the outcome as Daniel did.

The Literal City Of Babylon At The Time Of The END
There is a literal city "Babylon" at The Time Of The END.
It is the greatest city on earth in the greatest nation on earth,
Which it has always been throughout the ages,
And it is destroyed by the Antichrist and the ten kings he rules over,
At the end of The Great Tribulation.

CHRISTIANS, THE SCAPEGOAT FOR A LOST AND DYING WORLD

Christians Will Be Hated By All Nations
Christians will be hated by all nations
For the same reason that Christ Jesus was hated;
They declare to the world that what they do is evil and against the God of Heaven.
Christians will be hated by all nations because all nations belong to the devil
And the only entity standing in the way of their complete domination
Is the Church of Christ Jesus under the direction of the Holy Spirit.
As the deception of the devil increases
The social, political and economic systems of the world fall apart
And the plight of mankind becomes more desperate,
Christians will become the "scapegoat,"
And will be blamed for the social, political and economic woes of the world.
This phenomenon is well underway in every nation on earth.

Today, the judgment of God is on the social, political and economic systems
Of every nation of the face of the earth, because of their ungodliness,
Revealing their emptiness.
Under the deception of Satan they have ignored and forsaken the God of Heaven,
And have gone their own way, which only leads to their destruction.
They are murderers, extortioners, thieves and liars.
They demand their abortions, sacrificing their own children to the god of this world.
They demand their homosexuality, adultery, fornication and lewdness
Which in turn, demands God's ever increasing judgment.
They demand satisfaction of their ever increasing lust of the flesh,
And lust of the eyes.
They demand their false religions which tell them what they want to hear,
And ignore and malign the God of Heaven.
They adore their idols of persons who are ungodly people, lost and without hope.
They exult in their material possessions
And what they see themselves as having accomplished.
They are intoxicated with their power and prestige
They exult in their technology, their "savior."
All of which are at stake in their eyes,
As the world economic system devolves into a hopeless mess of their own making,
Under the deception of Satan.

Who Is To Blame?
Christians, the thorn in the side of the world;
The ones who keep lifting up Christ Jesus
As the only Way, the only Truth and the only LIFE.
Christians, who follow Christ Jesus the archenemy of the devil,

39

The Season Of The Last Generation

CHRISTIANS THE SCAPEGOAT FOR A LOST AND DYING WORLD

Who currently rules the world; who is the god of this world.
The ones who deny that everyone goes to heaven when they die,
But insist that eternal life is found by receiving Christ Jesus alone,
And His sacrifice on the cross of Calvary;
Being washed in His blood, being immersed in His Spirit,
And allowing Christ Jesus to live in and through them.

The Attack On Christians
Will Bring About The Apostasy / Rebellion
Within The Church of God

As the social, political and economic condition of the world deteriorates,
The attack on Christians will intensify.
This pressure will cause the false prophets and apostates within the Church
To arise and spread their deadly prophecies, and apostasies;
That all is well, and that God is on their side.
These false prophets and apostates, leaders within the Church,
Will justify the practices of the world with their
I'm OK, your OK, "lets all get along" position.
This direct opposition to God, His Christ and His Scriptures,
This is the "Apostasy / Rebellion" within the Church.
God, then, removes the Holy Spirit from the earth,
Which removes all restraint from the ungodly,
Allowing Satan to reveal his Antichrist
And to set up his "image" within the Church
And require that everyone worship the "image."
This is "The Abomination That Causes Desolation."
This act ignites The Great Tribulation,
The final judgment of God upon a world,
Whose sinfulness is beyond redemption.

JESUS CAME
TO BRING DIVISION AND FIRE

Jesus said: *'I have come to bring fire on the earth,*
And how I wish it were already kindled! But I have a baptism to undergo,
And how distressed I am until it is completed!
Do you think I came to bring peace on earth?
No, I tell you, but division.
From now on there will be five in one family divided against each other,
Three against two and two against three.
They will be divided, father against son and son against father,
Mother against daughter and daughter against mother, mother-in-law against
Daughter-in-law and daughter-in-law against mother-in-law.' (Luke 12:49-53)

The whole world belongs to Satan at this time
Except those who have given their lives to Christ Jesus.
When Jesus came, He came with the fire of God to destroy the devils work,
To set the captives free.
The devil does not let go easily and this causes division.
The Church of God is the focus of Satan's deception.
Throughout history the Church of God, over time, slips into the devil's camp.
When the fire of God shows up their is conflict;
In "The Season Of The Last Generation" there is the "Apostasy / Rebellion,"
As Christ Jesus steps into His Church and declares and demonstrates the Truth,
Through His Bride.
Just as in His day, He stepped into the midst of the Jewish religious environment
And caused havoc; His presence demanded a verdict
On the part of every Jewish person, and everyone made their choice;
Christ was crucified, but His Church was born.
In 70 A.D., having forsaken their Messiah,
The Jewish people were dispersed throughout the world, their Temple destroyed.

Likewise, The Bride of Christ will come on the scene;
Into the existing religious environment, in the fullness of Christ,
With the same charisma and presence as Christ.
She will cause the same reaction in that environment
As did Christ Jesus in His day,
Because it is the Spirit of Christ in Her that causes the stir and division.
The very presence of The Bride of Christ will demand a verdict,
You are either for Christ or not, you either gather with him or you scatter.
Every person who claims the name of Christ will be forced to make a choice.
For three and one-half years she will minister.
At the end of which, the name of Jesus, will be on every heart mind and mouth,
Every man women and child, throughout the whole world.

HE WHO IS NOT WITH ME IS AGAINST ME

Jesus said:
He who is not with me is against me,
And he who does not gather with me scatters.
And so I tell you, every sin will and blasphemy will be forgiven men,
But the blasphemy against the Spirit will not be forgiven.
Anyone who speaks a word against the Son of Man will be forgiven,
But anyone who speaks against the Holy Spirit will not be forgiven,
Either in this age or in the age to come.

Make a tree good and its fruit will be good,
Or make a tree bad and its fruit will be bad,
For a tree is recognized by its fruit.
You brood of vipers, how can you who are evil say anything good?
For out of the overflow of the heart the mouth speaks.
The good man brings good things out of the good stored up in him,
And the evil man brings evil things out of the evil stored up in him.
But I tell you that men will have to give an account on the day of judgment
For every careless word they have spoken.
For by your words you will be acquitted,
And by your words you will be condemned. *(Matthew 12:30-37)*

Jesus said:
Watch out for false prophets.
They come to you in sheep's clothing, but inwardly they are ferocious wolves.
By their fruit you will recognize them.
Do people pick grapes from thornbushes, or figs from thistles?
Likewise every good tree bears good fruit,
But a bad tree bears bad fruit,
A good tree cannot bear bad fruit, and a bad tree cannot bear good fruit.
Every tree that does not bear good fruit is cut down and thrown into the fire.
Thus, by their fruit you will recognize them. (Matthew 7:15-20)

The false prophets, the apostates and the rebellious in the Church of God,
In The Season Of The Last Generation will be against Christ,
And will scatter His people.
They are bad trees with bad fruit.
Their careless words will condemn them.
They are a brood of vipers and of the devil.
Nevertheless, like their master, Satan, they masquerade as angels of light.

The Season Of The Last Generation

Jesus describes further the Apostates and Rebellious in the Church of God:

Though seeing, they do not see; though hearing, they do not hear or understand.
In them is fulfilled the prophecy of Isaiah:
You will be ever hearing but never understand;
You will be ever seeing but never perceiving.
For this people's heart has become calloused;
They hardly hear with their ears, and they have closed their eyes.
Otherwise they might see with their eyes, hear with their ears,
Understand with their hearts and turn, and I would heal them. (Matthew 13:13-15)

And why do you break the command of God for the sake of your tradition?
For God said, 'Honor your father and mother'
And anyone who curses his father or mother must be put to death.
But you say that if a man says to his father or mother,
'Whatever help you might otherwise have received from me
Is a gift devoted to God,'
He is not to 'honor his father' with it.
Thus you nullify the word of God for the sake of your tradition.
You hypocrites! Isaiah was right when he prophesied about you:

'These people honor me with their lips, but their hearts are far from me.
They worship me in vain; their teachings are but rules taught by men.'
(Matthew 15:3-9)

Every plant that my heavenly Father has not planted will be pulled up by the roots.
Leave them; they are blind guides.
If a blind man leads a blind man, both will fall into a pit. (Matthew 15:13-14)

When evening comes, you say,
'It will be fair weather, for the sky is red and overcast,'
You know how to interpret the appearance of the sky,
But you cannot interpret the signs of the times.
A wicked and adulterous generation looks for a miraculous sign,
But none will be given it except the sign of Jonah. (Matthew 16:2-4)

[This generation needs to be able to interpret the signs of our times.
The Bride of Christ will correctly interpret
The sign of The Season Of The Last Generation.
The wicked and adulterous within the Church will not.]

In the time of Christ, the tax collectors and the prostitutes,
The worst of society, entered the Kingdom of God before the religious leaders:

I tell you the truth, the tax collectors and the prostitutes

The Season Of The Last Generation

HE WHO IS NOT WITH ME IS AGAINST ME

Are entering the Kingdom of God ahead of you.
For John came to you to show you the way of righteousness,
And you did not believe him,
But the tax collectors and the prostitutes did.
And even then, after you saw this, you did not repent and believe him.
(Matthew 21:31-32)

We can expect the same situation to repeat itself
In The Season Of The Last Generation.
No generation has had the Word of God available to them like this generation.
When Christ Jesus reveals His Bride to this generation they will be dumbfounded.
They will treat Her just as the religious leaders did Christ in His day.
This truth can be seen in the reaction of the Church of God
To every God sent Revival; it renounced them.

The Bride of Christ will invite the Church of God and this generation
To the Wedding Banquet of Christ Jesus
And most will refuse to come.
See the parable of the Wedding Banquet, Matthew 22:1-14.
However, just as in the parable, many sinners will accept the invitation.
Many who are first, will be last and many who are last, will be first.

THE APOSTASY / THE REBELLION

Matthew 24:10-11

Jesus said:

At that time (The Season Of The Last Generation) *many will turn away from the faith*
And will betray and hate each other,
And many false prophets will appear and deceive many people.

From the beginning of the New Testament Books
Satan has infiltrated the Church of God, masquerading as an angel of light.
This can be seen in the betrayal of Christ Jesus by Judas Iscariot.
It can be seen in the letters of the first Apostles and their warnings.
It can be seen in the Seven Letters to the Seven Churches in the Book of Revelation.
The Apostasy / Rebellion in The Season Of The Last Generation
Is the final attempt by Satan to destroy the plan a purpose of Christ Jesus.
And he fails.

The Church of God is the primary target for Satan.
He controls the rest of the world like puppets on strings.
If Satan can prevail against the Church of God he has achieved his objective;
To take all of mankind to hell with him.
However, he cannot prevail against the Church of God;
Those who allow Christ to live in and through them;
Christ is incomparably greater than the devil.

The Parable Of The Weeds (Matthew 13:24-30)

Jesus told them another parable:

The kingdom of heaven is like a man who sowed good seed in his field.
But while everyone was sleeping,
His enemy came and sowed weeds among the wheat, and went away.
When the wheat sprouted and formed heads, then the weeds also appeared.

The owner's servants came to him and said,
'Sir, didn't you sow good seed in your field?'
'Where then did the weeds come from?'
'An enemy did this,' he replied.
The servants asked him, 'Do you want us to go and pull them up?'

'No,' he answered, 'because while you are pulling the weeds,
You may root up the wheat with them.
Let both grow together until the harvest.
At that time I will tell the harvesters:
First collect the weeds and tie them in bundles to be burned,
Then gather the wheat and bring it into my barn.'

APOSTASY / REBELLION

**We can see from this parable that the Church of God will have "weeds" in it,
Until the final harvest takes place.
The "weeds" in the Church of God produce the Apostasy / Rebellion.**

We learn about the Apostasy /Rebellion in the following Scriptures:

Daniel 8:10-12

It (the kingdom of the Beast) *grew until it reached the host of the heavens,
And it threw some of the starry host* (leaders of the Church) *down to the earth
And trampled on them.
It set itself up to be as great as the Prince of the host* (Christ Jesus);
It took away the daily sacrifice (the worship of Christ Jesus)
From him (Christ),
And the place of his sanctuary (the Church) *was brought low.*
Because of rebellion,
The host of the saints and the daily sacrifice (worship of Christ)
Were given over to it (the kingdom of the Beast).
It prospered in everything it did, and truth was thrown to the ground.

The Rebellion Occurs (2 Thessalonians 2:1-12)

*Concerning the coming of the Lord Jesus Christ
And our being gathered to him, we ask you brothers,
Not to become easily unsettled or alarmed by some prophecy, report or letter
Supposed to have come from us, saying that the day of the Lord has already come.*

*Don't let anyone deceive you in any way, for that day will not come,
Until **the rebellion occurs** and the man of lawlessness is revealed,
The man doomed to destruction.
He opposes and exalts himself over everything that is called God or is worshiped,
And even sets himself up in God's temple, proclaiming himself to be God.*

*Don't you remember that when I was with you I used to tell you these things?
And now you know what is holding him back,
So that he may be revealed at the proper time.
For the secret power of lawlessness is already at work;
But the one who now holds it back will continue to do so
Till he (the Holy Spirit) is taken out of the way.*

**Today, people are trying to identify the Antichrist.
However, the apostle Paul tells us that the man of lawlessness,
The Antichrist, will not be revealed
Until the Holy Spirit is taken out of the way.
It is probable that the Antichrist remains unknown
Until he is finally revealed and there is no question as to who he is.**

The Season Of The Last Generation

Let's look at what other Scriptures teach us about the "weeds,"
That produce the Apostasy / Rebellion
That takes place at the Time Of The END,
The Season Of The Last Generation

1 Timothy 4:1-5
The Spirit clearly says that in later times some will abandon the faith
And follow deceiving spirits and things taught by demons.
Such teaching comes through hypocritical liars,
Whose consciences have been seared as with a hot iron.
They forbid people to marry and order them to abstain from certain foods,
Which God created to be received with thanksgiving
By those who believe and who know the truth.
For everything God Created is good,
And nothing is to be rejected if it is received with thanksgiving,
Because it is consecrated by the word of God and prayer.

Matthew 16:11-12
Jesus told His disciples:
But be on your guard against the yeast of the Pharisees and Sadducees.
(That is the teaching of the Pharisees and Sadducees;
Rules and regulations that have no basis in Scripture and often contradict Scripture.)

Colossians 2:8
The apostle Paul tells the Colossians:
See to it that no one takes you captive through hollow and deceptive philosophy,
Which depends on human tradition and the basic principles of this world
Rather than on Christ.

Hebrews 13:9
Do not be carried away by all kinds of strange teachings.

Matthew 15:8
Jesus said:
These people honor me with their lips, but their hearts are far from me.
They worship me in vain; their teachings are but rules taught by men.

1 Timothy 6:3
If anyone teaches false doctrines
And does not agree to the sound instruction of our Lord Jesus Christ
And to Godly teaching, he is conceited and understands nothing.

2 Timothy 4:3
For the time will come when men will not put up with sound doctrine.
Instead, to suit their own desires,
They will gather around them a great number of teachers
To say what their itching ears want to hear.
They will turn their ears away from the truth and turn aside to myths.

Titus 1:10-11
For there are many rebellious people, mere talkers and deceivers,
Especially those of the circumcision group.
They must be silenced, because they are ruining whole households
By teaching things they ought not to teach and that for the sake of dishonest gain.

2 Peter 2:1
But there were also false prophets among the people,
Just as there will be false teachers among you.
They will secretly introduce destructive heresies,
Even denying the sovereign Lord who bought them—
Bringing swift destruction on themselves.
Many will follow their shameful ways and will bring the way of truth into disrepute.
In their greed these teachers will exploit you with stories they have made up.
Their condemnation has long been hanging over them,
And their destruction has not been sleeping.

Matthew 7:15
Jesus said: *Watch out for false prophets.*
They come to you in sheep's clothing, but inwardly they are ferocious wolves.
By their fruit you will recognize them.

Mark 13:22-23
For false Christs and false prophets will appear and perform signs and miracles
To deceive the elect—if that were possible.
So be on your guard; I have told you everything ahead of time.

Characteristics of the Apostasy / Rebellion
1. Many will turn away from the faith and betray and hate each other. Many false prophets will appear and deceive many people.
2. Some will abandon the faith and follow deceiving spirits and things taught by demons. This teaching will come through hypocritical liars, whose consciences have been seared as with a hot iron.
3. They forbid people to marry and order them to abstain from certain foods.
4. Truth is thrown to the ground.
5. Teaching, rules and regulations that have no basis in Scripture.

6. Teachers will come with hollow and deceptive philosophy that depends on human tradition and the basic principles of this world rather than on Christ.
7. Strange teachings.
8. Rules will be taught by men, with no heart connection to Jesus.
9. False doctrines will be taught.
10. Men will turn to teachers with unsound doctrine to satisfy their itching ears.
11. Talkers and deceivers teaching things they ought not to teach for the sake of dishonest gain.
12. False prophets, will introduce destructive heresies, even denying the Lord; exploiting people with stories they have made up for greed.
13. False prophets will come in sheep's clothing, that are inwardly ferocious wolves.
14. False Christ's and false prophets will appear and perform signs and miracles to deceive the elect—if that were possible, which it is not.

The Pharisees Are Examples Of False Teachers
The Seven Woes (Matthew 23:1-36)

[Since there is nothing new under the sun and since history repeats itself, Characteristics of the Pharisees as false teachers will be in practice today.]

Then Jesus said to the crowds and to his disciples:
'The teachers of the law and the Pharisees sit in Moses' seat.
So you must obey them and do everything they tell you.
But do not do what they do, for they do not practice what they preach.
They tie up heavy loads and put them on men's shoulders,
But they themselves are not willing to lift a finger to move them.

Everything they do is done for men to see:
They make their phylacteries wide and the tassels of their prayer shawls long;
They love the place of honor at banquets
And the most important seats in the synagogues;
They love to be greeted in the marketplaces and to have men call them 'Rabbi.'

But you are not to be called 'Rabbi,'
For you have only one Master and you are all brothers.
And do not call anyone on earth 'father,'
For you have one Father and he is in heaven.
Nor are you to be called 'teacher,' for you have one Teacher, the Christ.
The greatest among you will be your servant.
For whoever exalts himself will be humbled,
And whoever humbles himself will be exalted.

Woe to you, *teachers of the law and Pharisees, you hypocrites!*
You shut the kingdom of heaven in men's faces.

49

The Season Of The Last Generation

APOSTASY / REBELLION

You yourselves do not enter, nor will you let those enter who are trying to.

Woe to you, *teachers of the law and Pharisees, you hypocrites!*
You travel over land and sea to win a single convert, and when he becomes one,
You make him twice as much a son of hell as you are.

Woe to you, *blind guides!*
You say, 'If anyone swears by the temple, it means nothing;
But if anyone swears by the gold of the temple, he is bound by his oath.
You blind fools! Which is greater:
The gold, or the temple that makes the gold sacred?
You also say, 'If someone swears by the altar, it means nothing;
But if anyone swears by the gift on it, he is bound by his oath.'
You blind men! Which is greater: the gift, or the altar that makes the gift sacred?
Therefore, he who swears by the altar swears by it and by everything on it.
And he who swears by the temple swears by it and by the one who dwells in it.
And he who swears by heaven swears by God's throne and by the one who sits on it.

Woe to you, *teachers of the law and Pharisees, you hypocrites!*
You give a tenth of your spices—mint, dill and cummin.
But you ignore the more important matters of the law—
Justice, mercy and faithfulness.
You should have practiced the latter, without neglecting the former.
You blind guides! You strain out a gnat but swallow a camel.

Woe to you, *teachers of the law and Pharisees, you hypocrites!*
You clean the outside of the cup and dish,
But inside they are full of greed and self-indulgence.
Blind Pharisee! First clean the inside of the cup and dish,
And then the outside also will be clean.

Woe to you, *teachers of the law and Pharisees, you hypocrites!*
You are like whitewashed tombs,
Which look beautiful on the outside
But on the inside are full of dead men's bones and everything unclean.
In the same way, on the outside you appear to people as righteous
But on the inside you are full of hypocrisy and wickedness.

Woe to you, *teachers of the law and Pharisees, you hypocrites!*
You build tombs for the prophets and decorate the graves of the righteous.
And you say, 'If we had lived in the days of our forefathers,
We would not have taken part with them in shedding the blood of the prophets.'
So you testify against yourselves
That you are the descendants of those who murdered the prophets.
Fill up, then, the measure of the sin of your forefathers!

The Season Of The Last Generation

You snakes! You brood of vipers! How will you escape being condemned to hell?
Therefore I am sending you prophets and wise men and teachers.
Some of them you will kill and crucify;
Others you will flog in your synagogues and pursue from town to town.
And so upon you will come all the righteous blood that has been shed on earth,
From the blood of Zechariah son of Berakiah,
Whom you murdered between the temple and the altar.
I tell you the truth, all this will come upon this generation.

O Jerusalem, Jerusalem, you who kill the prophets and stone those sent to you,
How often I have longed to gather your children together,
As a hen gathers her chicks under her wings, but you were not willing.
Look, your house is left to you desolate.
For I tell you, you will not see me again until you say,
'Blessed is he who comes in the name of the Lord.'

The Pharisees Diligently Study the Scriptures
But Fail To Recognize Christ Jesus (John 5:31-40)

If I testify about myself, my testimony is not valid.
There is another who testifies in my favor
And I know that his testimony about me is valid.

You have sent to John and he has testified to the truth.
Not that I accept human testimony; but I mention it that you may be saved.
John was a lamp that burned and gave light,
And you chose for a time to enjoy his light.

I have testimony weightier than that of John
For the very work that the Father has given me to finish,
And which I am doing, testifies that the Father has sent me.
And the Father who sent me has himself testified concerning me.
You have never seen his form, nor does his word dwell in you,
For you do not believe the one he sent.
You diligently study the Scriptures
Because you think that by them you possess eternal life.
These are the Scriptures that testify about me,
Yet you refuse to come to me to have life.

Israel, the "Church" in the time of Christ, failed to recognized their Messiah.
Since the resurrection of Christ Jesus,
God has sent many Holy Spirit driven Revivals to His Church.
In fact, the only thing that has kept the Church alive
Are the Revivals that God has sent.
However, the Church has resisted and failed to recognize most of these Revivals,
They were received, only by a remnant who recognized the voice of their God.

The Season Of The Last Generation

This pattern continues to this day.
Steven, just before he was stoned declared
That the Jews always resisted the Holy Spirit.
This was the pattern of Israel, the "Church" of the Old Testament,
And it is the pattern of the Church of Christ Jesus in the New Testament,
From the time of His resurrection on.

Today, the Church of God will be given a Final Revival.
Christ Jesus is raising up His Bride to minister in His fullness.
She will stand before the Church of God and the world
And declare and demonstrate the Glory of Christ.

In fact, She will be the catalyst for the Apostasy / Rebellion.
She will be the One who draws the line: Choose Life or choose death.
She will not allow, as Christ Jesus did not allow, any wiggle room.
You are either for Christ Jesus or you are against Him;
You either loose your life for His sake or you have no life;
You must take up your cross daily and follow Him or you have no life.

The False Church
The "Church" in the time of Christ Jesus said
That if they had lived in the time of the prophets of old
They would not have killed them as their ancestors had.
This same "Church" proceeded to kill the Prophet of prophets, the Christ of God.

Christ Jesus said to the Pharisees:
Woe to you, because you build tombs for the prophets
And it was your forefathers who killed them.
So you testify that you approve of what your forefathers did,
They killed the prophets, and you build their tombs.
Because of this, God in his wisdom said,
'I will send them prophets and apostles,
Some of whom they will kill and others they will persecute.'
Therefore this generation will be held responsible
For the blood of all the prophets that has been shed
Since the beginning of the world,
From the blood of Abel to the blood of Zechariah,
Who was killed between the altar and the sanctuary.
Yes, I tell you, this generation will be held responsible for it all. (Luke 11:47-51)

However, the "Church" of the time of Christ Jesus was not the True Church.
It was a False Church, claiming God, but belonging to the devil.

Christ Jesus gathered a Remnant out of the False Church
That heard the voice of God and were true to Him.

The Season Of The Last Generation

These are those who received Christ Jesus, included the first apostles
And those who received Christ at Pentecost and thereafter.
God always preserves a Remnant, in every generation, for His glory.
In every generation there is also a False Church
That pretends to belong to Christ but in reality belongs to the devil.
The wheat and the tares grow up together until God separates them.

The Season Of The Last Generation
Is the final separation of the wheat and the tares.

The True Church was in trouble before the last apostle died,
As can be seen from the seven letters to the seven churches.
By the time of Wycliffe, Hus, Luther and others around the 1500's
The "Church" was in desperate straights and almost dead.
God then raised up men and women to begin the restoration of the Truth
To the True Church.
The "restoration" began around the 1500's and continues to this day;
God restoring the "Truth" to His Church.

God has sent Revivals to every generation
To prevent His Church from slipping back Into apathy and apostasy.
Every Revival has received persecution from the False Church.
Every subsequent generation has been given more of His Truth.
God's Final Revival is about to begin.
Christ Jesus will reveal His Bride in His fullness
And this will bring great consternation to the False Church.
It will be exposed for what it is, "False," a pretender.
The "Apostasy / Rebellion" of The Season Of The Last Generation
Will expose the False Church;
She will be seen for what she is "naked," and without Christ.

The Gates Of Hell Will Not Prevail
Against The Church Of Christ Jesus

As Christ Jesus said, the gates of hell will not prevail against His Church;
The True Church of the Living God, The Bride of Christ.
It will including all those who have been true to their God
From the beginning of Scriptural history until today.

THE UNEXPECTED TRAP

Jesus said about a specific day:
Be careful, or your hearts will be weighed down with dissipation, drunkenness
And the anxieties of life,
And <u>that day</u> will close on you unexpectedly like a trap.
For it will come upon all those who live on the face of the whole earth.
Be always on the watch,
And pray that you may be able to escape all that is about to happen,
And that you may be able to stand before the Son of Man. (Luke 21:34-36)

Just as God has been working throughout these last two days, or 2,000 years,
Satan has also been working;
Bringing the final phase of his deception to its conclusion,
Knowing his time is short to accomplish his purpose.
Mankind is the proverbial frog in the pot,
The temperature has been steadily rising and is about to boil,
And they are about to be plunged into The Great Tribulation.

Satan has been preparing for his day since the ascension of Christ Jesus.
The day of Satan, the day his Antichrist takes control, is a trap for all mankind.
It will be a day when everything will change, socially, politically, and economically.
As God has been preparing a Bride for His Son, for eternal LIFE,
Satan has been preparing mankind to receive his Antichrist, his "mark,"
His bride, the prostitute, "Babylon," and eternal damnation.

For virtually all of mankind, the day will come unexpectedly, like a trap.
But Satan has prepared for this day for 2,000 years.
Because of the increase of wickedness, the love of most will have grown cold.
The heart of mankind without Christ will be weighed down with dissipation,
Drunkenness and the anxieties of life.
The increase in wickedness
Will be fueled by the social, political and economic unrest
And uncertainty in the world,
And the "Apostasy / Rebellion" in the Church of God.
God then removes the Holy Spirit from the earth.
Out of this chaos, Satan reveals his Antichrist, the Beast,
And sets up the "Abomination That Causes Desolation,"
Which is the "image" of the Beast in the Church of God.
Then every person will be required to worship the "image"
And received his "mark"or die.

When this occurs, all restraint is gone
And Satan proceeds with the killing of God's saints

One World Order, One World Leader:
The New Tower Of Babel: The Trap
For a long time the world has been busy constructing
The modern, international version of the ancient tower of Babel;
The coming together of the nations;
Relying on the wisdom of man, the end thereof is death.
They have been pushing the God of Heaven out of their cultures
And pursued their own man exalting, Satan inspired agenda;.
The lust of the flesh, the lust of the eyes and the pride of life.

Some time ago I heard of a statement attributed to a French diplomat
Who said, something like this:
'If a man could be found,
Who had the solution to the worlds social, political and economic problems,
Be he God or be he the devil the world would serve him.'

This would seem to be a prophetic concept for sure,
Because the Scripture teaches that at The Time of The END
The whole world will worship and serve the devil.
The world has always been in the control of the devil,
But at The Time of The END, it will be completely unmasked;
The Holy Spirit will be removed; the trap will be sprung.
Satan will have his day, but The Day of the Lord will put him to an end.

The Theology Of Satan
Satan has ingrained his theology into mankind
To the point of utter and complete blindness.
His theology is the lust of the flesh, the lust of the eyes
And the pride in what one possesses and has accomplished.
With his theology he has seduced virtually all of mankind.
Christ Jesus said that the flesh counts for nothing;
Satan says the flesh counts for everything.

The theology of Satan is in practice everywhere you look today.
It is "modern" idolatry.
It is personified in "Babylon" the greatest city of the greatest nation on earth.
The bride of Satan.
Every city of the world wants to be like "Babylon" and are in fact "Little Babylons."
The godless people of the world lust after their idols,
In the form of persons, material possessions, political and social power.
Appearance is everything, the God of Heaven forgotten.
They are puppets on the strings of Satan the ruler of their world.
By their actions they demand the judgment of God.

God's Wrath Against Mankind (Romans 1:18-32)

The wrath of God is being revealed from heaven
Against all the godlessness and wickedness of men
Who suppress the truth by their wickedness,
Since what may be known about God is plain to them,
Because God has made it plain to them.
For since the creation of the world God's invisible qualities--
His eternal power and divine nature--
Have been clearly seen, being understood from what has been made,
So that men are without excuse.
For although they knew God, they neither glorified him as God
Nor gave thanks to him, but their thinking became futile
And their foolish hearts were darkened.
Although they claimed to be wise, they became fools
And exchanged the glory of the immortal God
For images made to look like mortal man and birds and animals and reptiles.

Therefore God gave them over in the sinful desires of their hearts to sexual impurity
For the degrading of their bodies with one another.
*They exchanged the truth of God for a **lie**,*
And worshiped and served created things rather than the Creator--
Who is forever praised. Amen.

Because of this, God gave them over to shameful lusts.
Even their women exchanged natural relations for unnatural ones.
In the same way the men also abandoned natural relations with women
And were inflamed with lust for one another.
Men committed indecent acts with other men,
And received in themselves the due penalty for their perversion.

Furthermore, since they did not think it worthwhile to retain the knowledge of God,
He gave them over to a depraved mind, to do what ought not to be done.
They have become filled with every kind of wickedness, evil, greed and depravity.
They are full of envy, murder, strife, deceit and malice.
They are gossips, slanderers, God-haters, insolent, arrogant and boastful;
They invent ways of doing evil;
They disobey their parents; they are senseless, faithless, heartless, ruthless.
Although they know God's righteous decree
That those who do such things deserve death,
They not only continue to do these very things
But also approve of those who practice them.

[Here the apostle Paul describes the condition of the world today.
The wrath of God is being revealed from Heaven everyday
Against the wickedness in the world.

56

The Season Of The Last Generation

The world today, is speeding toward God's final judgment,
Like lemmings toward the edge of the cliff.]

Because of These The Wrath of God Is Coming (Colossians 3:5-11)
Put to death, therefore, whatever belongs to your earthly nature:
Sexual immorality, impurity, lust, evil desires and greed, which are idolatry.
Because of these, the wrath of God is coming.
You used to walk in these ways, in the life you once lived.
But now you must rid yourselves of all such things as these:
Anger, rage, malice, slander, and filthy language from your lips.
Do not lie to each other, since you have taken off your old self with its practices
And have put on the new self, which is being renewed in knowledge
In the image of its Creator.
Here there is not Greek or Jew, circumcised or uncircumcised,
Barbarian, Scythian, Slave or free, **but Christ is all**, *and is in all.*

[The sinfulness of mankind in the face of a holy God, demands His judgment,
An His final judgment will come at the appointed time.]

Godlessness In The Last Days (2 Timothy 3:1-7)
But mark this: There will be terrible times in the last days.
People will be lovers of themselves, lovers of money, boastful, proud, abusive,
Disobedient to their parents, ungrateful, unholy, without love, unforgiving,
Slanderous, without self-control, brutal, not lovers of the good,
Treacherous, rash, conceited.
Lovers of pleasure rather than lovers of God--
Having a form of godliness but denying its power.
Have nothing to do with them.

They are the kind who worm their way into homes
And gain control over weak-willed women, who are loaded down with sins
And are swayed by all kinds of evil desires,
Always learning but never able to acknowledge the truth.

[This description by Paul aptly describes the time we are living in.
This is what is seen on television every day,
Both in serial programs and on the news.
Churches, claiming Christ, are defying The Word of God by their practices,
Which renders them powerless with God and in defiance of Him.]

The Man Of Lawlessness (2 Thessalonians 2:1-12)
Concerning the coming of the Lord Jesus Christ
And our being gathered to him, we ask you brothers,
Not to become easily unsettled or alarmed by some prophecy, report or letter
Supposed to have come from us, saying that the day of the Lord has already come.

The Season Of The Last Generation

Don't let anyone deceive you in any way, for <u>that day</u> will not come,
*<u>Until the rebellion occurs</u> and **the man of lawlessness** is revealed,*
The man doomed to destruction.
He opposes and exalts himself over everything that is called God or is worshiped,
And even sets himself up <u>in God's temple</u>, proclaiming himself to be God.

Don't you remember that when I was with you I used to tell you these things?
And now you know what is holding him back,
So that he may be revealed at the proper time.
For the secret power of lawlessness is already at work;
But the one who now holds it back will continue to do so
<u>Till he (the Holy Spirit) is taken out of the way</u>.
*And then the **lawless one** will be revealed,*
Whom the Lord Jesus will over throw with the breath of his mouth
And destroy by the splendor of his coming.
*The coming of the **lawless one** will be in accordance with the work of Satan*
Displayed in all kinds of <u>counterfeit</u> miracles, signs and wonders,
And every sort of evil that deceives those who are perishing.
They perish because they refused to love the truth and so be saved.

*For this reason God sends them **a powerful delusion***
*So that they will believe **the lie***
And so that all will be condemned who have not believed the truth
But have delighted in wickedness.

[According to the apostle Paul,
The Day Of The Lord will not come until the "man of lawlessness,"
The Beast, the Antichrist is revealed.
Before this happens the Holy Spirit is taken out of the way
And Satan has complete rule over mankind.
The Beast sets up his "image" in the Church of God,
Claiming to be God and deceiving mankind
With <u>counterfeit</u> miracles, signs and wonders.
God allows this <u>powerful delusion</u> for those who have delighted in wickedness.]

The Coming Of The Lord (1 Thessalonians 4:13-18, 5:1-11))
Brothers, we do not want you to be ignorant about those who fall asleep,
Or to grieve like the rest of men, <u>who have no hope</u>.
We believe that Jesus died and rose again
And so we believe that God will bring with Jesus
*Those who have fallen asleep **in him**.*
According to the Lord's own word, we tell you that we who are still alive,
Who are left till the coming of the Lord,
Will certainly not precede those who have fallen asleep.

The Season Of The Last Generation

For the Lord himself will come down from heaven, with a loud command,
With the voice of the archangel and with the trumpet call of God,
And the dead in Christ will rise first.
After that, we who are still alive and are left
Will be caught up with them in the clouds to meet the Lord in the air.
And so we will be with the Lord forever,
Therefore encourage each other with these words.

[The Lord comes with a loud command and the trumpet call of God
At the end of The Great Tribulation an just before The Battle of Armageddon.
At that time the only saints left on earth alive are those in the desert
Who have been protected by God; the "Woman," the Bride of Christ.]

Now, brothers, about times and dates we do not need to write to you,
For you know very well that the <u>day of the Lord</u>
Will come like a thief in the night.
While people are saying, 'Peace and safety,'
Destruction will come on them suddenly, as labor pains on a pregnant woman,
And they will not escape.

[At this time, just before The Great Tribulation begins,
The Bride of Christ will be gone; the trouble maker will be gone.
Satan will have enthroned the "image" of his Antichrist in God's Church,
And every person will worship "one god," Satan.
There will be the minor inconvenience of killed the remaining Christians.
It will appear to the world that peace has finally come.
The world will be united under one leader, one god, one economic system.]

But you, brothers, are not in darkness
So that this day should surprise you like a thief.
You are all sons of the light and sons of the day.
We do not belong to the night or to the darkness.
So then, let us not be like others, who are asleep,
But let us be alert and self-controlled.
For those who sleep, sleep at night, and those who get drunk, get drunk at night.
But since we belong to the day, let us be self-controlled, putting on faith
And love as a breastplate, and the hope of salvation as a helmet.

For God did not appoint us to suffer wrath
But to receive salvation through our Lord Jesus Christ.

He died for us so that, whether we are awake or asleep,
We may live together with him.
Therefore encourage one another and build each other up,
Just as in fact you are doing.

The Season Of The Last Generation

The Day Of The Lord (2 Peter 3:1-13)
Dear friends, this is now my second letter to you.
I have written both of them as reminders to stimulate you to wholesome thinking.
I want you to recall the words spoken in the past by the holy prophets
And the command given by our Lord and Savior through your apostles.

First of all, you must understand that in the last days scoffers will come,
Scoffing and following their own evil desires.
They will say, 'Where is this coming' he promised?
Ever since our fathers died, everything goes on as it has
Since the beginning of creation.

But they deliberately forget that long ago by God's word the heavens existed
And the earth was formed out of water and with water.
By water also the world of that time was deluged and destroyed.
By the same word the present heavens and earth are reserved for fire,
Being kept for the day of judgment and destruction of ungodly men.

But do not forget this one thing, dear friends:
With the Lord a day is like a thousand years,
And a thousand years like a day.
The Lord is not slow in keeping his promise, as some understand slowness.
He is patient with you, not wanting anyone to perish,
But everyone to come to repentance.
But the day of the Lord will come like a thief.
The heavens will disappear with a roar;
The elements will be destroyed by fire,
And the earth and everything in it will be laid bare.

Since everything will be destroyed in this way, what kind of people ought you to be?
You ought to live holy and godly lives
As you look forward to the day of God and speed its coming.
That day will bring about the destruction of the heavens by fire,
And the elements will melt in the heat.
But in keeping with his promise we are looking forward to a new heaven
And a new earth, the home of the righteousness.

In The Last Times There Will Be Scoffers (Jude 17-18)
But, dear friends, remember what the apostles of our Lord Jesus Christ foretold.
They said to you,

'In the last times there will be scoffers
Who will follow their own ungodly desires.'

These are the men who divide you, who follow mere natural instincts

And do not have the Spirit.

Love, For The Day Is Near (Romans 13:8-14)
Let no debt remain outstanding, except the continuing debt to love one another,
For he who loves his fellow man has fulfilled the law.
The commandments, 'Do not commit adultery,' 'Do not murder,' Do not steal,'
'Do not covet,' and whatever other commandment there may be,
Are summed up in this one rule:

'Love your neighbor as yourself.'
Therefore love is the fulfillment of the law.
And do this, understanding the present time
The hour has come for you to wake up from your slumber,
Because our salvation is nearer now than when we first believed.

The day of Satan occurs when the man of lawlessness appears,
The Antichrist, the Beast, the son of Satan.
This is the "trap" for most of mankind.
The day of the Lord is when the judgment of God commences upon the earth.
At this time, the judgment of God comes like a thief in the night,
While the people of the earth are expecting peace and safety.
The day of the Lord concludes at The Battle of Armageddon;
With the Second coming of Christ Jesus;
With the defeat of the Satan, his Antichrist and all the nations of the earth.

THE TRAP OF NOAH'S DAY

Jesus compared the days of Noah to the "Season" preceding The Great Tribulation.
Noah preached to his generation for a long time prior to the flood,
Just as the Church of God has preached to every generation
Since the ascension of Christ Jesus.

By the time of Noah, Satan had deceived the whole world of that time.
The wickedness of man had reached the point of no return.
Mankind had become so wicked that it was irreversible;
They were "trapped" in their sin.
This is what happens at The Time of the END.
This is a testament to the effectiveness of Satan's deception.

God Made A Covenant With Noah
Noah was a righteous man, blameless among the people of his time,
And he walked with God. (Genesis 6:9)

God made a covenant with Noah;
God promised to save Noah and his family through the ark.
Today, God has made a covenant with His people,
He has placed His laws in their minds and written them upon their hearts
(Jeremiah 31);
He has promised eternal life to those who "know" Him.
In God's New Covenant, those who receive His Christ,
Are washed in the blood of Christ, and their sins are forgiven.

God Instructed Noah How To Build The Ark Of Salvation
God gave Noah very specific instructions as to how to build the ark of salvation.
Today, we have the teachings of Christ Jesus, His apostles and all of Scripture.
Our salvation is found in following those teachings
By the power of the indwelling Holy Spirit.

Noah Knew That The World Of His Day Would Be Destroyed
God told Noah that He was going to bring a flood
That would destroy the world of Noah's day.
Today, God has told us that this world we are living in will be destroyed.

God Gave The World Of Noah's Day Many Years To Turn To Him
It took Noah many years to build the ark as his neighbors watched on.
The construction of the ark was in itself "preaching" to those who watched.
God has given the world of our day two thousand years to turn to Him;
For two thousand years Christians have preached to this world in word and deed.

The Season Before The Flood

Finally the ark was finished.
The completion of the ark is similar to the "Season" before The Great Tribulation.
It would have taken Noah sometime to collect and march
The great contingent of animals and supplies into the ark.
This time would be similar to the ministry of The Bride of Christ
For the three and one-half years preceding The Great Tribulation.
The Bride of Christ will invite whosoever will to the Christ of God.
Then will come the inescapable Tribulation.
The door to salvation, except to die for Christ, will be shut,
Just as surely as God shut the door behind Noah and his family.

When God shut the door to the ark,
To those outside, it was like any other day.
For seven days the door of the ark was shut
With Noah and his family and all of the animals inside.
Imagine the mocking of those outside.
However, on the seventh day it began to rain and did not stop.
The rains continued for forty days,
Until every living thing outside the ark was killed.
It will be like this once The Great Tribulation begins, there will be no escape.

The Bride of Christ will be taken into the desert to a place prepared by God.
The people of the world will wonder for a time where they have gone.
Shortly thereafter it will become clear to them that The Great Tribulation has begun.
The difference with this time and Noah's time
Is that every living person that finds themselves in The Great Tribulation
Will be given the opportunity to die for Christ and live eternally;
They will be given the opportunity to refuse the "mark" of the Beast and be killed,
But live eternally in the presence of Christ Jesus.

The Wickedness of Man In Noah's Day

The Lord saw how great man's wickedness on the earth had become,
And that every inclination of the thoughts of his heart
Was only evil all the time.
The Lord was grieved that he had made man on the earth,
And his heart was filled with pain.
So the Lord said,
'I will wipe mankind, whom I have created, from the face of the earth—
Men and animals and creatures that move along the ground, and birds of the air--
For I am grieved that I have made them.'
But Noah found favor in the eyes of the Lord. (Genesis 6:5-8)

Now the earth was corrupt in God's sight and was full of violence.
God saw how corrupt the earth had become,

The Season Of The Last Generation

For all the people on earth had corrupted their ways.
So God said to Noah,
'I am going to put an end to all people,
For the earth is filled with violence because of them.
I am surely going to destroy both them and the earth.' (Genesis 6:11-13)

The Time Of The END Will Be As The Days Of Noah

Jesus said:
No one knows about that day or hour,
Not even the angels in heaven, nor the Son, but only the Father.
As it was in the days of Noah, so it will be at the coming of the Son of Man.
For in the days before the flood, people were eating and drinking,
Marrying and giving in marriage, up to the day Noah entered the ark;
And they knew nothing about what would happen until the flood came
And took them all away. *(Matthew 24:36-39)*

Likewise The Great Tribulation will come
And "trap" virtually all of mankind into its terror and darkness.

THE TRAP OF SODOM AND GOMORRAH

In the days of Abraham,
The sin and wickedness of Sodom and Gomorrah had reached the point of no return,
And they were trapped in their sinfulness,
Just as will happen in the "Season" before The Great Tribulation.

The Outcry Against Sodom And Gomorrah

The the Lord said (to Abraham),
The outcry against Sodom and Gomorrah is so great and their sin so grievous
That I will go down and see if what they have done is as bad as the outcry
That has reached me. If not then I will know. (Genesis 18:20-21)

Two angels from God go to the city of Sodom to witness first hand its condition.
Abraham's nephew, Lot, was at the city gate when the angels came.
Knowing what the Sodomites would do to the two angels,
Lot invited them to stay at his home, to protect them. However:

Before they had gone to bed, all the men from every part of the city of Sodom—
Both young and old—surrounded the house.
They called to Lot.
'Where are the men who came to you tonight?
Bring them out to us so that we can have sex with them.'

Lot went outside to meet them and shut the door behind him and said,
'No, my friends. Don't do this wicked thing.
Look, I have two daughters who have never slept with a man.
Let me bring them out to you , and you can do what you like with them.
But don't do anything to these men,
For they have come under the protection of my roof.'

'Get out of our way,' they replied. And they said,
'This fellow came here as an alien, and now he wants to play the judge!
We'll treat you worse than them.'
They kept bringing pressure on Lot
And moved forward to break down the door.

But the men inside reached out and pulled Lot back into the house
And shut the door.
Then they struck the men who were at the door of the house,
Young and old with blindness so that they could not find the door.
(Genesis 19:4-11)

The Season Of The Last Generation

Such was the wickedness of Sodom in Lot's day,
And their wickedness brought the judgment of God upon them.

The Lord Rained Down Burning Sulfur On Sodom And Gomorrah
Then the Lord rained down burning sulfur on Sodom and Gomorrah--
From the Lord out of the heavens.
Thus he overthrew those cities and the entire plain,
Including all those living in the cities--
And also the vegetation in the land. (Genesis 19:23-25)

Ezekiel give us a glimpse of the sin of Sodom:
'Now this was the sin of your sister Sodom;
She and her daughters were arrogant, overfed and unconcerned;
They did not help the poor and needy.
They were haughty and did detestable things before me.
Therefore I did away with them as you have seen.' (Ezekiel 16:49-50)

Ungodly people call good, evil and evil, good.
But what they determine is irrelevant to God, they are deceived by Satan.
God has a standard that He has made clear in His Word.
When wickedness reaches the point of no return,
All that remains is His judgment.
That is what happens at The Time of the END.
God devastates the earth and mankind and puts an end to sin.
In the END sin will have no place in God's creation.

THE ALLEGORY
OF UNFAITHFUL JERUSALEM

When I first read Ezekiel 16, I was stunned by its parallel to America.
It also has a parallel to every nation with a Christian heritage.
It is the story of these nations in The Season Of The Last Generation.

The word of the Lord came to me:
'Son of man, confront Jerusalem (America) with her detestable practices and say,
This is what the Sovereign Lord says to Jerusalem (America):
Your ancestry and birth were in the land of the Canaanites;
Your father was an Amorite and your mother a Hittite.
On the day you were born your cord was not cut,
Nor were you washed with water to make you clean,
Nor were you rubbed with salt or wrapped in cloth.
No one looked on you with pity
Or had compassion enough to do any of these things for you.
Rather, you were thrown out into the open field,
For on the day you were born you were despised.

Then I passed by and saw you kicking about in your blood
And as you lay there in your blood I said to you, 'Live!'
I made you grow like a plant of the field.
You grew up and developed and became the most beautiful of jewels.
Your breasts were formed and your hair grew, you who were naked and bare.

Later I passed by,
And when I looked at you and saw that you were old enough for love,
I spread the corner of my garment over you and covered your nakedness.
I gave you my solemn oath and entered into a covenant with you,
Declares the sovereign Lord, any you became mine.

I bathed you with water and washed the blood from you and put ointments on you.
I clothed you with an embroidered dress and put leather sandals on you.
I dressed you in fine linen and covered you with costly garments.
I adorned you with jewelry: I put a ring in your nose, earrings on your ears
And a beautiful crown on your head.
So you were adorned with gold and silver; your clothes were of fine linen
And costly fabric and embroidered cloth.
Your food was fine flour, honey and olive oil.
You became very beautiful and rose to be a queen.
And your fame spread among the nations on account of your beauty,
Because the splendor I had given you made your beauty perfect,
Declares the Sovereign Lord.

The Season Of The Last Generation

But you trusted in your beauty and used your fame to become a prostitute.
You lavished your favors on anyone who passed by and your beauty became his.
You took some of your garments to make gaudy high places,
Where you carried on your prostitution.
Such things should not happen, nor should they ever occur.
You also took the fine jewelry I gave you, the jewelry made of my gold and silver,
And you made for yourself male idols and engaged in prostitution with them.
And you took your embroidered clothes to put on them,
And you offered my oil and incense before them.
Also the food I provided for you—
The fine flour, olive oil and honey I gave you to eat—
You offered as fragrant incense before them.
That is what happened, declares the Sovereign Lord.

And you took your sons and daughters whom you bore to me
And sacrificed them as food to the idols.
Was your prostitution not enough?
You slaughtered my children and sacrificed them to the idols.
In all your detestable practices and your prostitution
You did not remember the days of your youth,
When you were naked and bare, kicking about in your blood. (Ezekiel 16:1-22)

A REBELLIOUS NATION

(Isaiah 1 speaks not only to Israel of his day,
But to America and every nation with a Christian heritage.)

Hear, O heavens! Listen, O earth! For the Lord has spoken:
'I reared children and brought them up, but they have rebelled against me.
The ox knows his master, the donkey his owners manger,
But Israel (American and every nation with a Christian heritage)
Does not know, my people do not understand.'

Ah, sinful nation, a people loaded with guilt, a brood of evildoers,
Children given to corruption.
They have forsaken the Lord; they have spurned the holy One of Israel
And turned their backs on him.

Why should you be beaten anymore?
Why do you persist in rebellion? Your whole head is injured,
Your whole heart afflicted.
From the sole of your foot to the top of your head there is no soundness--
Only wounds and welts and open sores,
Not cleansed or bandaged or soothed with oil.

Your country is desolate, your cities burned with fire;
Your fields are being stripped by foreigners right before you,
Laid waste as when overthrown by strangers.
The Daughter of Zion (America and every nation with a Christian heritage)
Is left like a hut in a field of melons, like a city under siege.

Unless the Lord Almighty had left us some survivors,
We would have become like Sodom, we would have been like Gomorrah.

Hear the word of the Lord, you rulers of Sodom
(Rulers of America and every nation with a Christian heritage);
Listen to the law of our God, you people of Gomorrah!
'The multitude of your sacrifices—what are they to me?' says the Lord.
'I have more than enough of burnt offerings,
Of rams and the fat of fattened animals;
I have not pleasure in the blood of bulls and lambs and goats.
When you come to meet with me, who has asked this of you,
This trampling of my courts?
Stop bringing meaningless offerings!
Your incense is detestable to me.
New Moons, Sabbaths and convocations--
I cannot bear your evil assemblies.
Your New Moon festivals and your appointed feasts my soul hates.
They have become a burden to me;

The Season Of The Last Generation

I am weary of bearing them.
When you spread out your hands in prayer, I will hid my eyes from you;
Even if you offer many prayers, I will not listen.
Your hand are full of blood; wash and make yourselves clean.
Take your evil deeds our of my sight!
Stop doing wrong, learn to do right!
Seek justice, encourage the oppressed.
Defend the cause of the fatherless, plead the case of the widow.

'Come now, let us reason together,' says the Lord.
'Though your sins are like scarlet, they shall be white as snow;
Though they be red as crimson, they shall be like wool.
If you are willing and obedient, you will eat the best from the land;
But if you resist and rebel, you will be devoured by the sword.'
For the mouth of the Lord has spoken.

See how the faithful city (America and every nation with a Christian heritage)
Has become a harlot!
She once was full of justice; righteousness used to dwell in her--But now murderers!
Your silver has become dross, your choice wine is diluted with water.
Your rulers are rebels, companions of thieves; they all love bribes
And chase after gifts.
They do not defend the cause of the fatherless;
The widow's case does not come before them.
Therefore the Lord, the Lord almighty, the Mighty One of Israel, declares:
'Ah, I will get relief from my foes and avenge myself on my enemies.
I will turn my hand against you;
I will thoroughly purge away your dross and remove your impurities.
I will restore your judges as in days of old, your counselors as at the beginning.
Afterward you will be called The City of Righteousness, The Faithful City.'
(At the end of The Battle of Armageddon,
Christ Jesus will rule and reign for a thousand years.)
Zion (The City of God, The Bride of Christ, The Israel of God, The Church of Christ),
Will be redeemed with justice, her penitent ones with righteousness.
But rebels and sinners will both be broken together,
And those who forsake the Lord will perish.
(This includes every person and nation that does not receive the Christ of God.)

'You will be ashamed because of the sacred oaks in which you have delighted,
You will be disgraced because of the gardens you have chosen.
You will be like a garden without water.
The mighty man will become tinder and his work a spark;
Both will burn together with no one to quench the fire.'

JESUS INSTRUCTIONS FOR HIS BRIDE

The instructions that Jesus gives His Bride in The Season Of The Last Generation
Will be similar to those He gave to the twelve when He sent them out.
Except this time they are to go into all the world.

As you go, preach this message: 'The Kingdom of Heaven is near,'
Heal the sick, raise the dead, cleanse those who have leprosy, drive out demons.
Freely you have received, freely give. (Matthew 10:7-8)

Whatever town or village you enter, search for some worthy person there
And stay at his house until you leave.
As you enter the home, give it your greeting.
If the home is deserving, let your peace rest on it;
If it is not, let your peace return to you.
If anyone will not welcome you or listen to your words,
Shake the dust off your feet when you leave that home or town.
I tell you it will be more bearable for Sodom and Gomorrah on the day of judgment
Than for that town.

I am sending you out like sheep among wolves.
Therefore be as shrewd as snakes and as innocent as doves.
But be on your guard against men;
They will hand you over to the local councils
And flog you in their synagogues (Churches).
On my account you will be brought before governors and kings
As witnesses to them and to the Gentiles.
But when they arrest you do not worry about what to say or how to say it.
At that time you will be given what to say, for it will not be you speaking,
But the Spirit of your Father speaking through you.

Brother will betray brother to death, and a father his child;
Children will rebel against their parents and have them put to death.
All men will hate you because of me,
But he who stands firm to the end will be saved.
When you are persecuted in one place, flee to another.
I tell you the truth, you will not finish going through the cities of Israel
Before the Son of Man comes. *(Matthew 10:11-23)*

[Here it is clear that Jesus is speaking to The Bride of Christ,
In The Season Of The Last Generation, as well as to His disciples in His day.]

The Season Of The Last Generation

JESUS INSTRUCTIONS FOR THE BRIDE OF CHRIST

A student is not above his teacher, not a servant above his master.
It is enough for the student to be like his teacher,
And the servant to be like his master.
If the head of the house has been called Beelzebub,
How much more the members of his household!

So do not be afraid of them.
There is nothing concealed that will not be disclosed,
Or hidden that will not be made known.
What I tell you in the dark, speak in the daylight;
What is whispered in your ear, proclaim from the housetops.
Do not be afraid of those who kill the body but cannot kill the soul.
Rather, be afraid of the one who can destroy the soul and body in hell.
Are two sparrows sold for a penny?
Yet not one of them will fall to the ground apart from the will of your Father.
And even the very hairs of your head are all numbered.
So don't be afraid; you are worth more than many sparrows.

Whoever acknowledges me before men,
I will also acknowledge him before my Father in heaven.
But whoever disowns me before men,
I will disown him before my Father in heaven.

Do not suppose that I have come to bring peace to the earth.
I did not come to bring peace, but a sword.
For I have come to turn a man against his father,
A daughter against her mother,
A daughter-in-law against her mother-in-law--
A man's enemies will be the members of his own household.

Anyone who loves his father or mother more than me is not worthy of me;
Anyone who loves his son or daughter more than me is not worthy of me;
And anyone who does not take his cross and follow me is not worthy of me.
Whoever finds his life will lose it, and whoever loses his life for my sake will find it.

He who receives you receives me,
And he who receives me receives the one who sent me.
Anyone who receives a prophet because he is a prophet
Will receive a prophet's reward,
And anyone who receives a righteous man because he is a righteous man
Will receive a righteous man's reward.
And if anyone gives a cup of cold water to one of these little ones
Because he is my disciple, I tell you the truth, he will certainly not lose his reward.
(Matthew 10:24-42)

The Season Of The Last Generation

[Once again Jesus is talking about two different time frames at the same time.
He is talking about the day He is living in, and The Season Of The Last Generation,
And all the time in between.]

THE BRIDE OF CHRIST

In The Season Of The Last Generation a Remnant, a Bride
Will arise out of the Church of God.
The woman with a holy, unquenchable passion for her God.
She will confirm a covenant with Christ Jesus for seven years
According to Daniel 9:27;
She will minister in the fullness of Christ for the three and one-half years
That precede The Great Tribulation.

Her appearance will be as startling to the Church of God
As was the appearance of Christ Jesus in His day.
She will be persecuted by the False Church just as Christ Jesus was.
The False Church will attempt to kill her, but fail.
She will be taken into a desert place prepared for her by God,
And protected for the three and one-half years of The Great Tribulation.

Christ Jesus was slain from the foundation of the world.
He was slain to bring forth a Bride.
After His death and resurrection
God the Father has sent the Holy Spirit to obtain a Bride for His Son.
The Bride He will marry and who will be ONE with Him for eternity.
In what follows we will look at what the Scriptures teach us about this Bride.

In Ephesians 5:25-27, Paul says:
*'Husbands love your wives as Christ loved the church
And gave himself up for her to make her holy,
Cleansing her by the washing with water through the word,*
***And to present her to himself as a radiant church,
Without stain or wrinkle or any other blemish.'***

In 2 Corinthians 11:2, Paul says:
*'I promised you to one husband, to Christ,
So that I might present you as a pure virgin to him.'*

In Isaiah 62 the Lord speaks of His zeal for His Bride:
*'For Zion's sake I will not keep silent,
For Jerusalem's sake I will not remain quiet,
Till her righteousness shines out like the dawn,
Her salvation like a blazing torch.*

*The nations will see your righteousness, and all kings your glory;
You will be called by a new name that the mouth of the Lord will bestow.
You will be a crown in the Lord's hand,
A royal diadem in the hand of your God.*

The Season Of The Last Generation

No longer will they call you deserted, or name your land Desolate.
But you will be called Hephzibah, and your land Beulah;
For the Lord will take delight in you, and your land will be married.
As a young man marries a maiden, so will your sons marry you;
As a bridegroom rejoices over his bride,
So will your God rejoice over you.

I have posted watchmen on your walls, O Jerusalem;
They will never be silent day or night.

You, who call on the Lord, give yourselves no rest,
And give him no rest till he establishes Jerusalem
And makes her the praise of the earth.'

Examples of women who were types of the Bride of Christ are as follows:

REBECAH
The young woman chosen by God to be the wife of Isaac,
Who bore Jacob, who is in the lineage of Christ Jesus,
And was a demonstrator of the attributes of the Bride of Christ Jesus. (Genesis 24)

MIRIAM
Miriam was a type of the Bride,
Leading the people of God into praise and worship of the Living God.
After the children of Israel had walked through the sea on dry land, it says:

Then Miriam the prophetess, Aaron's sister,
Took a tambourine in her hand, and all the women followed her
With tambourines and dancing.
Miriam sang to them;
'Sing to the Lord, for he is highly exalted
The horse and its rider he has hurled into the sea.' (Exodus 15:20-21)

Here Miriam is exhibiting the nature of the Bride.
She was a prophetess
And Scripture declares that Christ Jesus is the Spirit of prophesy.

DEBORA
Judges 4 is the account of Deborah.

Deborah, a prophetess, the wife of Lappidoth, was leading Israel
She held court under the Palm of Deborah between Ramah and Bethel
In the hill country of Ephraim, and the Israelites came to her
To have their disputes decided. (Exodus 4:4-5)

The Season Of The Last Generation

Deborah received a word from the Lord
That would save Israel out of the hand of their enemies,
And it required that she risk her life to carry it out.

RUTH
Ruth was a young woman who held steadfast to her faith in the face of hardship.
She obeyed her mother-in-law, a follower of God
And the Lord delivered Ruth and the mother-in-law from ruin.
The child that Ruth subsequently bore was in the lineage of Christ Jesus.
(The Book of Ruth)

ESTER
Ester was a young woman who risked her life to save the Israelites from extinction.
(The Book of Ester)

PROVERBS
In Proverbs we are introduced to "Wisdom", she;
A type of the Bride of Christ.

Wisdom calls aloud in the street
She raises her voice in the public squares;
At the head of the noisy streets she cries out,
In the gateways of the city she makes her speech:
How long will you simple ones love your simple ways?
How long will mockers delight in mockery
And fools hate knowledge?
If you had responded to my rebuke,
I would have poured out my heart to you
And made my thoughts known to you. (Proverbs 1:20-23)

The Wife of Noble Character
A wife of noble character who can find?
She is worth far more than rubies.
Her husband has full confidence in her and lacks nothing of value
She brings him good, not harm,
All the days of her life. (Proverbs 31:10-12)

THE SONG OF SONGS
Introduces us to the intimacy of Christ Jesus and His Bride.
The Song of Songs is a book that describes the love affair
Between Christ Jesus and His Bride.
The following are paraphrases from that book, put into a poetic form:

Who is this?
(Christ Jesus speaking of His Bride)

The Season Of The Last Generation

Who is this who appears like the dawn?
Fair as the moon
Bright as the sun
Majestic as the stars
All beautiful you are
There is no flaw in you
You have stolen my heart my sister my bride
With one glance of your eyes

How delightful is your love my darling
Better that wine, fragrant as perfume
You are a garden fountain
A well of flowing water
There is no one like you
You have stolen my heart my sister my bride
With one glance of your eyes

For the King is captivated by your beauty
The King is captivated by your love

I Belong to You My King
(The Bride of Christ speaking to her King)

I belong to you my King
My desire is for you alone
Place me like a seal over you heart
Like a brand upon your arm

For my love for you is as strong as death
It burns like a blazing fire
An ocean of water cannot quench my love
A river cannot wash it away

All the wealth of this world
Is as nothing compared to our love
Every delicacy both new and old
I have brought to you my love

For my love for you is as strong as death
It burns like a blazing fire
An ocean of water cannot quench my love
A river cannot wash it away

Come away with me my lover my friend
Let me be your complete contentment

The Season Of The Last Generation

Come away with me my lover my friend
Let me be your complete contentment
Let me be your complete contentment

Arise My Darling
(Christ Jesus calling to His Bride)

Arise my darling my beautiful one
Arise my darling my beautiful one
Come with me
The winter is past and the rains are all gone
The flowers appear, the time for singing has come

Arise my darling my beautiful one
Arise my darling my beautiful one
Come with me

The cooing of doves is heard in our land
The fig tree forms its early fruit
The blossoming vines spread their fragrance
Arise and come with me

Arise and come
Arise and come
Arise and come with me

Arise and come
Arise and come
Arise and come with me

**Christ Jesus has been calling forth His Bride in every generation.
The relationship between Christ Jesus and His Bride
Is an exquisite, beautiful, intimate relationship.**

**A comparison would be the courtship between a man and a woman
When it is as God intended.**

This is the nature of the relationship that Christ Jesus has with His Bride.

THE MARRIAGE OF CHRIST JESUS AND HIS BRIDE
*Then I heard what sounded like a great multitude,
Like the roar of rushing waters
And like loud peals of thunder, shouting:
'Hallelujah!'
For the Lord our God almighty reigns*

And give Him the glory!
<u>*For the wedding of the Lamb has come*</u>
<u>*And His bride had made herself ready.*</u>
Fine linen, bright and clean, was given to her to wear.
(Fine linen stands for the righteous acts of the saints.)

Then the angel said to me,
'Write: Blessed are those who are invited to the wedding supper of the Lamb!'
And he added, 'Theses are the true words of God.'
(Revelation 19:6-9)

THE NEW JERUSALEM, THE BRIDE OF CHRIST
John goes on to say:
'Then I saw a new heaven and a new earth,
For the first heaven and the first earth had passed away,
And there was no longer any sea.
I saw the Holy City, the New Jerusalem,
Coming down out of heaven from God,
<u>*Prepared as a Bride beautifully dressed for her husband*</u>
And I heard a loud voice from the throne saying,
'Now the dwelling of God is with men.
They will be His people,
And God Himself will be with them and be their God.
He will wipe every tear from their eyes.
There will be no more death or mourning or crying or pain,
For the old order of things has passed away.'
He who was seated on the throne said,
'I am making everything new!'
Then he said, 'Write this down,
For these words are trustworthy and true.'

He said to me:
'It is done.
I am the Alpha and the Omega, the Beginning and the End
To him who is thirsty I will give to drink without cost
From the spring of the water of LIFE.
He who overcomes will inherit all this,
And I will be his God and he will be my son.
But the cowardly, the unbeliever, the vile, the murderers
The sexually immoral,
Those who practice magic arts, the idolaters and all liars--
Their place will be in the fiery lake of burning sulfur.
This is the second death.'

One of the seven angels who had the seven bowls full of the seven last plagues

The Season Of The Last Generation

THE BRIDE OF CHRIST

Came and said to me,

'Come and I will show you the Bride, the wife of the Lamb.'
And he carried me away in the Spirit to a mountain great and high,
And showed me the Holy City, Jerusalem,
Coming down out of heaven from God
It shown with the glory of God,
And its brilliance was like that of a very precious jewel,
Like jasper, clear as crystal.
It had a great, high wall with twelve gates,
And with twelve angels at the gates.
On the gates were written the names of the twelve tribes of Israel.
There were three gates on the east, three on the north, three on the south
And three on the west.
The wall of the city had twelve foundations,
And on them were the names of the twelve apostles of the Lamb.

The angel who talked with me had a measuring rod of gold to measure the city,
Its gates and its wall.
The city was laid out like a square, as long as it was wide.
He measured the city with the rod and found it to be 1,400 miles in length,
And as wide and high as it is long.
He measured its wall and it was 200 feet thick,
By man's measurement, which the angel was using.
The wall was made out of jasper, and the city of pure gold, as pure as glass.
The foundations of the city walls were decorated with every kind of precious stone.
The first foundation was jasper, the second sapphire,
The third chalcedony, the forth emerald, the fifth sardonic, the sixth carnelian,
The seventh chrysolite, the eighth beryl, the ninth topaz, the tenth chrysoprase,
The eleventh jacinth, and the twelfth amethyst.
The twelve gates were twelve pearls, each gate made of a single pearl.
The street of the city was of pure gold like transparent glass.

I did not see a temple in the city,
Because the Lord God almighty and the Lamb are its temple.
The city does not need the sun or the moon to shine on it,
For the glory of God gives it light, and the Lamb is its lamp
The nations will walk by its light,
And the kings of the earth will bring their splendor into it.
On no day will its gates ever be shut,
For there will be no night there.
The glory and honor of the nations will be brought into it.
Nothing impure will ever enter it,
Nor will anyone who does what is shameful or deceitful,
But only those whose names are written in the Lamb's book of LIFE.'

(Revelation 21:1-27)

At the point in time spoken of here in Revelation 21:1-27
God has now achieved His purpose in creation,
He has redeemed a people to Himself,
And made them ONE with Himself, by the power of His Holy Spirit;
Living stones built together to comprise the City of God;

A Bride who has fully submitted Her will to His will;
A Bride who has made Her WAY, His WAY, Her TRUTH, His TRUTH
Her LIFE, His LIFE.
A Bride who is LOVE, as He is LOVE.
A Bride who is ONE with Christ Jesus.

THE ROMANCE OF ALL THE AGES
Is now consummated,
The Lord of Glory has His glorious Bride
A Bride commensurate with Himself in character and being
By the power of His Holy Spirit
And they live happily ever after

TODAY
Today God is calling a people to Himself;
Those who have ears to hear Him;
Those who hear His voice;
Those who worship God in Spirit and in Truth;
Who have been crucified with Christ and no longer live,
But Christ lives in and through them;
Those who have the humility of a child;
Those who have guarded their hearts;
Those who seek first the Kingdom of God above all else;
Those in whom the love of Christ lives;
Those who live in the Secret Place of the Most High God;
Those who know God and are known by God;
Those who possess eternal LIFE in the here and now;
Those who God honors with His anointing;
Those who do the will and works of Christ Jesus.

This people who God is raising up today
Will join those from all previous generations
Who made Him their LIFE;

A Bride who will come on the scene as Christ Jesus did
When His ministry began in Israel 2000 years ago;
Startling the whole religious community and the world;

The Season Of The Last Generation

THE BRIDE OF CHRIST

Shaking them out of their complacency;
Making it impossible to sit on the fence;
Making it impossible to be lukewarm;
Requiring that a choice be made;
Bringing the Word of God to LIFE;
Verifying its authenticity;
Revealing Christ Jesus in all His Glory.

The name of Jesus will be upon every heart mind and mouth,
Every man women and child,
In every place and every nation on the face of the earth,

And every person will be invited to make Christ Jesus
Their Savior, Lord and Bridegroom.
Isaiah speaks of the Bride of Christ:

'In that day the Lord Almighty
Will be a glorious crown, a beautiful wreath
For the remnant of his people
He will be a Spirit of justice
To Him who sits in judgment,
A source of strength
To those who turn back the battle at the gate.' (Isaiah 28:5-6)

Just before the end of time,
The Lord Almighty becomes a glorious crown, a beautiful wreath
For the remnant of His people, the Bride of Christ.
In the strength of her God,
She holds back the battle at the gate,
Until her mission is complete.
Her mission is to proclaim and demonstrate
The reality and power of Christ.

Ready or not, here I come
Give all glory to my Son
Get aboard the glory train
Give praise to His holy name

The wind of my Spirit is blowing over the land
Convicting souls, tell me where do you stand
This is the last and final call

82

The Season Of The Last Generation

THE BRIDE OF CHRIST

Love Jesus go tell all

Take your stand in the victory He won
Everyone else is going to be undone
Stand for Christ, you will not stand-alone
He's coming to take you home

MARANATHA, come soon Lord Jesus!
Your Bride awaits you!

THE FIRST WILL BE LAST AND THE LAST WILL BE FIRST

In the New Testament we are given a number of pictures
Of this amazing concept from the Word of God.
These are pictures of what will occur in The Season Of The Last Generation.
In this "Season" many will be first, though they are last
And many last, though they are first.
Every person will be "tested" by the Christ of God in this "Season,"
Their motivations and heart condition laid bare before Him.

After Christ Jesus told the rich young man
That if he wanted to be perfect he should sell all his possessions
And give them to the poor and follow Him.
The young man had walked away sad
Because he could not bring himself to do that since he was very wealthy.

Then Jesus said to his disciples,
'I tell you the truth, it is hard for a rich man to enter the kingdom of heaven.
Again I tell you, it is easier for a camel to go through the eye of a needle
Than for a rich man to enter the kingdom of God.

When the disciples heard this, they were greatly astonished and asked,
'Who then can be saved?'

Jesus looked at them and said,
'With man this is impossible, but with God all things are possible.'

[Every Christian can do the impossible through Christ in them.
They are able to sell all, follow Christ, and count it all joy.]

Peter answered him,
'We have left everything to follow you! What then will there be for us?'

Jesus said to them,
'I tell you the truth, at the renewal of all things,
When the Son of man sits on his glorious throne,
You who have followed me will also sit on twelve thrones,
Judging the twelve tribes of Israel.
And everyone who has left houses or brothers or sisters or father or mother
Or children or fields for my sake will receive a hundred times as much
And will inherit eternal life.
But many who are first will be last, and many who are last will be first.
(Matthew 19:23-30)

…IRST WILL BE LAST AND THE LAST WILL BE FIRST

…ing that many who come into the Kingdom first,
…s, will have a lesser reward
…ingdom at The Time Of The END.
…own challenges
…ed according to what they are asked to do for God,
…God.

…lity again
…in the vineyard.
…ers who worked only the last hours of the day
…ho worked the whole day.
…e whole day complained,
…wner had promised.

…orkers who worked only the last hours of the day
…orked the whole day. (Matthew 20:1-16)

…*nd the first will be last.' (Matthew 20:16)*

…essing and reward based on His perfect knowledge.

GOD OFFERS LIFE OR DEATH

The Offer Of Life Or Death (Deuteronomy 30:11-20)
Now what I am commanding you today
Is not too difficult for you or beyond your reach.
It is not up in heaven, so that you have to ask,
'Who will ascend into heaven to get it and proclaim it to us so we may obey it?'
Nor is it beyond the sea, so that you have to ask,
'Who will cross the sea to get it and proclaim it to us so we may obey it?'

See, I set before you today life and prosperity, death and destruction.
For I command you today to love the Lord your God,
To walk in his ways, and to keep his commands, decrees and laws;
Then you will live and increase,
And the Lord your God will bless you in the land you are entering to possess.

But if your heart turns away and you are not obedient,
And if you are drawn away to bow down to other gods and worship them,
I declare to you this day that you will certainly be destroyed.
You will not live long in the land you are crossing the Jordan to enter and possess.

This day I call heaven and earth as witnesses against you
*That I have set before you **life** and **death**, blessings and curses.*
***Now choose life**, so that you and your children may live*
And that you may love the Lord your God, listen to his voice, and hold fast to him.
***For the Lord is your life**,*
And he will give you many years in the land he swore to give to your fathers,
Abraham, Isaac and Jacob.

This promise from God is for every living person.

VISION OF THE BODY OF CHRIST AND END-TIME MINISTRIES

From book entitled PERTINENT PROPHECIES - I
By John M. and Dorthea M. Gardner
By permission given by Tommy Hicks, evangelist, July 25, 1961

My message begins July 25, 1961 about 2:30 in the morning at Winnipeg, Canada.
I had hardly fallen asleep
When the vision and the revelation that God gave me came before me.
The vision came three times, exactly in detail, the morning of July 25, 1961.
I was so stirred and so moved by the revelation
That this has changed my complete outlook upon the Body of Christ,
And the End-Time ministries.

The greatest thing that the church of Jesus Christ has ever been given
Lies straight ahead.
It is so hard to help men and women to realize and understand
The thing that God is trying to give to his people in the End-Times.

I received a letter several weeks ago from one of our native evangelists
Down in Africa, down in Nairobi.
This man and his wife were on their way to Tanganyika,
They came across a small village.
The entire village was evacuating because of a plague that had hit the village.
He came across natives that were weeping, and he asked them what was wrong.

They told him of their mother and father who had suddenly died,
And they had been dead for three days.
They had to leave.
They were afraid to go in; they were leaving them in the cottage.
He turned and asked them where they were.
They pointed to the hut and he asked them to go with him, but they refused.
They were afraid to go.

The native and his wife went to this little cottage
And entered in where the man and woman had been dead for three days.
He simply stretched forth his hand in the name of the Lord Jesus Christ,
And spoke the man's name and the woman's name and said,
"In the name of the Lord Jesus Christ, I command life to come back to your bodies."
Instantaneously these two heathen people
Who had never known Jesus Christ as their Savior
Sat up and immediately began to praise God.
The Spirit and the power of God came into the life of those people.

87

The Season Of The Last Generation

VISION OF THE BODY OF CHRIST AND END-TIME MINISTRIES

To us that may seem strange and a phenomenon,
But that is the beginning of these End-Time ministries.
God is going to take every man and every woman
And he is going to give them this outpouring of the Spirit of God.

In the book of Acts we read
"In the last days," God said, "I will pour out my Spirit upon all flesh."

I wonder if we realized what he meant when God said,
"I will pour out my Spirit upon all flesh."
I do not think I fully realize nor could I understand the fullness of it,
And then I read from the book of Joel:

"Be glad then, ye children of Zion, and rejoice in the Lord your God:
For he hath given you the former rain moderately,
And he will cause to come down for you the rain, the former rain,
And the latter rain..." (Joel 2:23).

It is not only going to be the rain, the former rain and the latter rain,
But he is going to give to his people in these last days
A double portion of the power of God!

As the vision appeared to me after I was asleep,
I suddenly found myself in a great high distance.
Where I was, I do not know.
But I was looking down upon the earth.
Suddenly the whole earth came into my view.
Every nation, every kindred, every tongue came before my sight
From the east and the west, the north and the south.
I recognized every country and many cities that I had been in,
And I was almost in fear and trembling as I beheld the great sight before me:
And at that moment when the world came into view,
It began to lightning and thunder.

As the lightning flashed over the face of the earth,
My eyes went downward and I was facing the north.
Suddenly I beheld what looked like a great giant,
And as I stared and looked at it, I was almost bewildered by the sight.
It was so gigantic and so great.
His feet seemed to reach to the north pole and his head to the south.
Its arms were stretched from sea to sea.
I could not even begin to understand whether this be a mountain or this be a giant,
But as I watched, I suddenly beheld a great giant.
I could see his head was struggling for life.
He wanted to live, but his body was covered with debris from head to foot,

The Season Of The Last Generation

VISION OF THE BODY OF CHRIST AND END-TIME MINISTRIES

And at times this great giant would move his body
And act as though it would even raise up at times.
And when it did, thousands of little creatures seemed to run away.
Hideous creatures would run away from this giant,
And when he would become calm, they would come back.

All of a sudden this great giant lifted his hand toward the heaven,
And then it lifted its other hand,
And when it did, these creatures by the thousands
Seemed to flee away from this giant and go into the darkness of the night.

Slowly this great giant began to rise and as he did,
His head and hands went into the clouds.
As he rose to his feet he seemed to have cleansed himself
From the debris and filth that was upon him,
And he began to raise his hands into the heavens as though praising the Lord,
And as he raised his hands, they went even unto the clouds.

Suddenly, every cloud became silver, the most beautiful silver I have ever known.
As I watched this phenomenon
It was so great I could not even begin to understand what I all meant.
I was so stirred as I watched it, and I cried unto the Lord and I said,
"Oh, Lord what is the meaning of this,"
And I felt as if I was actually in the Spirit
And I could feel the Presence of the Lord even as I was asleep.

And from those clouds suddenly there came great drops of liquid light
Raining down upon this mighty giant,
And slowly, slowly, this giant began to melt,
Began to sink itself in the very earth itself,
And as he melted, his whole form seemed to have melted upon the face of the earth,
And this great rain began to come down.
Liquid drops of light began to flood the very earth itself
And as I watched this giant that seemed to melt,
Suddenly it became millions of people over the face of the earth.
As I beheld the sight before me, people stood up all over the world!
They were lifting their hands and they were praising the Lord.

At that very moment there came a great thunder
That seemed to roar from the heavens.
I turned my eyes toward the heavens and suddenly I saw a figure in white,
In glistening white—the most glorious thing that I have ever seen in my entire life.
I did not see the face, but somehow I knew it was the Lord Jesus Christ,
And as he stretched forth his hand upon the nations
And the people of the world—men and women—as he pointed toward them,

The Season Of The Last Generation

VISION OF THE BODY OF CHRIST AND END-TIME MINISTRIES

This liquid light seemed to flow from his hands into them,
And those people began to go forth in the name of the Lord.

I do not know how long I watched it.
It seemed it went into days and weeks and months.
And I beheld this Christ as he continued to stretch forth his hand;
But there was a tragedy.
There were many people as he stretched forth his hand
That refused the anointing of God and the call of God.
I saw men and women that I knew.
People that I felt would certainly receive the call of God.
But as he stretched forth his hand toward this one and toward that one,
They simply bowed their head and began to back away, seemed to go into darkness.
Blackness seemed to swallow them everywhere.

I was bewildered as I watched it, but these people that he had anointed,
Hundreds of thousands of people all over the world,
In Africa, England, Russia, China, America, all over the world,
The anointing of God was upon these people
As they went forward in the name of the Lord.
I saw these men and women as they went forth.
They were ditch diggers, they were washerwomen, they were rich men,
They were poor men.
I saw people who were bound
With paralysis and sickness and blindness and deafness.
As the Lord stretched forth to give them this anointing,
They became well, they became healed, and they went forth!

And this is the miracle of it—this is the glorious miracle of it--
Those people would stretch forth their hands exactly as the Lord did,
And it seemed as if there was the same liquid fire in their hands.
As they stretched forth their hands they said,
"According to my word, be thou made whole."

As these people continued in this mighty end-time ministry,
I did not fully realize what it was, and I looked to the Lord and said,
"What is the meaning of this?" And he said,
"This is that which I will do in the last days.
I will restore all that the cankerworm, the palmerworm, the caterpillar--
I will restore all that they have destroyed.
This, my people, in the end times will go forth.
As a mighty army shall they sweep over the face of the earth."

As I was at a great height, I could behold the whole world.
I watched these people as they were going to and fro over the face of the earth.

The Season Of The Last Generation

VISION OF THE BODY OF CHRIST AND END-TIME MINISTRIES

Suddenly there was a man in Africa
And in a moment he was transported by the Spirit of God,
And perhaps he was in Russia, or China or America or some other place,
And vice versa.
All over the world these people went,
And they came through fire, and through pestilence, and through famine.
Neither fire nor persecution, nothing seemed to stop them.
Angry mobs came to them with swords and with guns.
And like Jesus, they passed through the multitudes and they would not find them,
But they went forth in the name of the Lord,
And everywhere they stretched forth their hands,
The sick were healed, the blind eyes were opened.
There was not a long prayer,
And after I had reviewed the vision many times in my mind,
And I thought about it many times, I realized that I never saw a church,
And I never saw or heard a denomination,
But these people were going in the name of the Lord of Hosts. Hallelujah!

As they marched forth in everything they did
As the ministry of Christ in the End-Times,
These people were ministering to the multitudes over the face of the earth.
Tens of thousands, even millions seemed to come to the Lord Jesus Christ
As these people stood forth and gave the message of the kingdom,
Of the coming kingdom, in this last hour.
It was so glorious,
But it seems as though there were those that rebelled,
And they would become angry
And they tried to attack those workers that were giving the message.

God is going to give to the world a demonstration in this last hour
As the world has never known.
These men and women are of all walks of life, degrees will mean nothing.
I saw these workers as they were going over the face of the earth.
When one would stumble and fall, another would come and pick him up.
There were no "big I" and "little you," but every mountain was brought low
And every valley exalted, and they seemed to have one thing in common--
There was a divine love, a divine love that seemed to flow forth from these people
As they worked together, and as they lived together.

It was the most glorious sight that I have ever known.
Jesus Christ was the theme of their life.
They continued and it seemed the days went by as I stood and beheld this sight.
I could only cry, and sometimes I laughed.
It was so wonderful as these people went throughout the face of the whole earth,
Bringing forth in this last end time.

The Season Of The Last Generation

VISION OF THE BODY OF CHRIST AND END-TIME MINISTRIES

As I watched from the very heaven itself,
There were times when great deluges of this liquid light
Seemed to fall upon great congregations,
And that congregation would lift their hands and seemingly praise God for hours
And even days as the Spirit of God came upon them.
God said, "I will pour out my Spirit upon all flesh,"
And that is exactly the thing,
And to every man and every woman that received this power,
And the anointing of God, the miracles of God, there was no ending to it.
We have talked about miracles. We have talked about signs and wonders,
But I could not help but weep as I read again this morning at 4 o'clock this morning
The letter from our native workers.
This is only the evidence of the beginning for one man,
A "do-nothing, and unheard-of,"
Who would go and stretch forth his hand and say,
"In the name of the Lord Jesus Christ, I command life to flow into your body."
I dropped to my knees and began to pray again, and I said,
"Lord, I know that this thing is coming to pass, and I believe it's coming soon!"

Suddenly there was another great clap of thunder,
That seemed to resound around the world,
And I heard again the voice, the voice that seemed to speak,
"Now this is my people. This is my beloved bride,"
And when the voice spoke, I looked upon the earth
And I could see the lakes and the mountains.
The graves were opened and people from all over the world,
The saints of all ages, seemed to be rising.
And as they rose from the grave,
Suddenly all these people came from every direction.
From the east and west, from the north and south,
And they seemed to be forming again this gigantic body.
As the dead in Christ seemed to be rising first, I could hardly comprehend it.
It was so marvelous. It was so far beyond anything I could ever dream or think of.

But as this body suddenly began to form, and take shape again,
It took shape again in the form of this mighty giant, but this time it was different.
It was arrayed in the most beautiful gorgeous white.
Its garments were without spot or wrinkle as its body began to form,
And the people of all ages seemed to be gathered into this body,
And slowly, slowly, as it began to form up unto the very heavens,
Suddenly from the heavens above, the Lord Jesus came, and became the head,
And I heard another clap of thunder that said,
"This is my beloved bride for whom I have waited.
She will come forth even tried by fire.
This is she that I have loved from the beginning of time."

The Season Of The Last Generation

VISION OF THE BODY OF CHRIST AND END-TIME MINISTRIES

As I watched, my eyes suddenly turned to the far north,
And I saw seemingly destruction: men and women in anguish and crying out,
And buildings in destruction.

Then I heard again, the fourth voice that said,
"Now is My wrath being poured out upon the face of the earth."
From the ends of the whole earth, the wrath of God seemed to be poured out
And it seemed that there were great vials of God's wrath
Being poured out upon the face of the earth.
I can remember it as though it happened a moment ago.
I shook and trembled as I beheld the awful sight of seeing the cities,
And whole nations going down into destruction.

I could hear the weeping and wailing. I could hear people crying.
They seemed to cry as they went into caves,
But the caves in the mountains opened up.

They leaped into water, but the water would not drown them.
There was nothing that could destroy them.
They were wanting to take their lives, but they could not.

Then again I turned my eyes to this glorious sight,
This body arrayed in beautiful white, shining garments.
Slowly, slowly, it began to lift from the earth, and as it did, I awoke.
What a sight I had beheld!
I had seen the End-Time ministries—the last hour.
Again on July 27, at 2:30 in the morning,
The same revelation, the same vision came again exactly as it did before.

My life has been changed as I realized that we are living in that End-Time,
For all over the world God is anointing men and women with this ministry.
It will not be doctrine. It will not be churchianity.
It is going to be Jesus Christ.
They will give forth the word of the Lord, and are going to say,
I heard it so many times in the vision, "and according to my word it shall be done."

Oh, my people, listen to me. According to my word, it shall be done.
We are going to be clothed with power and anointing from God.
We won't have to preach sermons,
We won't have to have persons heckle us in public.
We won't have to depend upon man, nor will we be denomination echoes,
But we will have the power of the living God.
We will fear no man, but will go in the name of the Lord of Hosts!

YOUR KINGDOM COME ON EARTH AS IN HEAVEN

This is what Christ Jesus taught His disciples to pray.
This prayer was not for the by and by but for the here and now.
Why do I say that?
Because Jesus said that the Kingdom of God had come upon them
When He performed His miracles;
It was a demonstration of the finger of God.
The miracles were the evidence
That God's Kingdom had come to earth as in Heaven
Where everything is supernatural.

Then Christ Jesus conferred His Kingdom on His disciples;
Incomprehensibly, He gave The Kingdom of Heaven,
His supernatural Kingdom to His disciples.
The Kingdom belonged to them; it was theirs.
He said it was inside them; yes, it was Christ in them.

We Know God's Kingdom Has Come To Earth As In Heaven When His Glory Is Manifested

After Christ Jesus left this earth,
The fact that His Kingdom had come to earth as in Heaven
Continued to be manifested, as demonstrated in the Book of Acts.
It continues to this day as recorded by history.
Every Revival in history demonstrated the reality of God's Glory
And the presence of His Kingdom on earth as in Heaven.

Glory Is The Atmosphere Of Heaven

In Heaven the atmosphere is Glory, created by the Presence of God.
It is pure and Holy as God is pure and Holy.
Like air is the atmosphere of earth, Glory is the atmosphere of Heaven.
It is completely supernatural
In Heaven there is nothing natural.

The Good News Is That God's Kingdom Has Come To Earth As In Heaven And Is Available To All

Christ Jesus said: 'Repent for the Kingdom of heaven is near.' (Matthew 4:17)
The Kingdom of God was near because Christ Jesus was near
And He embodied the Kingdom of God.
On The Day of Pentecost the Kingdom of God came to earth as in Heaven;
That is Christ, the Holy Spirit came and inhabited His people.

The Season Of The Last Generation

YOUR KINGDOM COME ON EARTH AS IN HEAVEN

God's Kingdom is the realm of His Spirit, the realm of His Glory.
It is supernatural, there is nothing natural about it.
It may be proclaimed by a man
But belief and confession can only be produced by God.
It is God, touching the heart of a man or woman and reveling Himself to them.
Out of this revelation they are able to believe and make their confession of faith.
This revelation is completely supernatural.

What does God say that the New Covenant is?
He tells us, that unlike the Old Covenant that remained in the natural,
In the New Covenant He places His law in our minds and writes it on our hearts;
This is a supernatural impartation done by God.

Getting saved entails a supernatural revelation from God.
That imparts belief, faith and Christ the Holy Spirit.
An impartation of His Kingdom on earth as in Heaven.

Christ Jesus says we are to pray,
To ask God to bring His Kingdom to earth as in Heaven;
That His will would be done on earth as in Heaven.
That everything we do on earth as as followers of Christ
Would be as it is done in Heaven;
That everything that happens in and through His people becomes supernatural.

When Christ Jesus sent His disciples out,
He sent them out to preach this message:
"The Kingdom of Heaven is near."
Today, we preach that the Kingdom of God is here.
He sent them out with His Glory, the Glory of His Kingdom.
He told them to heal the sick, raise the dead;
That what they were freely given (God's Kingdom Glory) they were to freely give.
This was before The Day of Pentecost;
It was an example of what was to happen, typically, after Pentecost;
It was an example of what did happen, typically, after Pentecost.
The Kingdom of God is available to all who come to Christ Jesus in faith.

Salvation Is Supernatural From The Beginning To The End
Every person who believes in their heart that God raised Christ Jesus from the dead
And makes a confession of that faith; that Christ Jesus is their Lord,
Is saved out of this world.
They are saved and are being saved as the apostle Paul said.
Now they must stand firm to the end to be finally saved.
They must overcome this world by the blood of the Lamb
And the word of their testimony.
All of this is made possible by Christ living in and through us;

The Season Of The Last Generation

YOUR KINGDOM COME ON EARTH AS IN HEAVEN

Christ in us, is the Kingdom of God in us, our hope of Glory.
We are saved clear through by the supernatural enablement of Christ in us.
We are saved by the grace of God, and not by works,
Least any man should attempt to boast;
There is no work of man that can accomplish this.
That would be the ultimate blasphemy.

How Does Anyone Know That God Is Present?
When The Glory Of His Kingdom Is Revealed!

God intended that this revelation of Himself and His Kingdom
Would be demonstrated through His people.
It was not to be simply words, but a demonstration of the power of God;
The power resident in His Kingdom;
God intended that the people of God reveal the tangible Presence of God
Through the Glory of His Kingdom, manifested.
Then everyone knows that the Kingdom of God has come to earth as in Heaven;
Then His will is done on earth as in Heaven.
Then the work of the devil is destroyed,
Which is what Christ Jesus came to do.
That is what Christ Jesus instructed His disciples to do.
Christ Jesus said the signs that would follow those who believe would include:
The casting out of demons, speaking in new tongues and healing the sick.
The Scriptures attest that after Pentecost, the disciples went out,
Preaching everywhere and the Lord worked with them
And confirmed His Word by the signs that accompanied the preaching.

The apostle Paul told the Corinthians:
**My message and my preaching were not with wise and persuasive words,
but with a demonstration of the Spirit's power,
So that your faith might not rest on men's wisdom, but on God's power.
(1 Corinthians 2:4)**

The Express Will Of God:
That His Kingdom Come To Earth As In Heaven

Christ Jesus said that the only people who go to Heaven when they die
Are those who have done the will of God.
**The simple prayer that Christ Jesus taught His disciples
Is the express will of God;**
That His Kingdom come and His will be done on earth as in Heaven;
That this be accomplished in and through His people;
That the lost might know that Christ Jesus reigns over all the earth.
This is all leading up to the Millennium, where The Kingdom of God comes to earth
As in Heaven for a thousand years, unhindered by the deception of the devil;
Where the Glory of God covers the earth as the water covers the sea.

96

When The Kingdom Of God Comes To Earth As In Heaven
The Work Of The Devil Is Destroyed
The devil has no access to the Kingdom of God in Heaven.
When the Kingdom of God Comes to earth as in Heaven, he is excluded;
He must stand down, stand back, and depart.
When the Kingdom of God comes to earth as in Heaven the strongman is bound
And rendered impotent.
He rules the world, for the time being,
But when God's Kingdom comes to earth as in Heaven he is rendered powerless.
Jesus said that the miracles that He did
Demonstrated that He had bound the strongman, the devil,
The perpetrator of all that is evil.
Christ Jesus took from the devil what he had previously stolen.
Christ Jesus restored sight, hearing, wellness, physical wholeness and even life itself.
When the Kingdom of God comes to earth as in Heaven,
It brings the wholeness of Heaven.
In the atmosphere of Heaven people are made whole again,
According to God's original intention.

Do you want to be made whole?
Get into the atmosphere of God's Glory, the atmosphere of Heaven.

Jesus came to destroy the devil's work.
The devil has perverted everything God intended for good.
Christ Jesus came to destroy this perversion,
By bringing His Kingdom to earth as in Heaven.

Christ Jesus Said That As The Father Sent Him,
He Now Sends Us
Christ Jesus has sent His people with the same equipment that He possessed;
As sheep among wolves, but with the power of His Kingdom;
The power and the Glory of God, the atmosphere of Heaven,
To destroy all the work of the devil.

The main tool the devil uses is his ability to deceive;
And this, supernatural, evil genius is a master at that among humans.
He has had 6,000 years of practice.
Nevertheless, Christ in His people is incomparably stronger than the devil.
We can do all things through Christ who strengthens us.
We can do exceedingly and abundantly above what we can think or ask
By the power of Christ in us.
We can declare the good news, that the Kingdom of God is here,
And we can demonstrate that fact just as Christ Jesus did.
This is the express will of God and the command of Christ Jesus.

The Season Of The Last Generation

We are to go into all the world and make disciples of all men,
Through the demonstration of the Kingdom of God,
So, that their faith would not rest on the words of man.
But on the power of God, as the apostle Paul said.

Speaking Against What Can Only Be Produced By God Is The Unforgivable Sin

Scripture teaches that when a person speaks against
What can only be produced by the Spirit of God, it is unforgivable,
Because you are speaking against God Himself.
You are speaking against what can only be produced by God.
The Pharisees did this when they claimed
That Christ Jesus drove out demons by the power of Beelzebub (the devil).

The Acts of Christ Jesus could only be produced by God Himself.
The Gospels portray the Acts of Christ Jesus.
Acts that can only be produced by God.
Unbelief, in the face of that produce by God, is unforgivable.
There is no hope for it. It is condemned and already dead.

God Sends His Kingdom To Earth As In Heaven To Produce Faith In The Lost

The Glory of God manifested; miracles, produce faith in unhardened hearts.
Christ Jesus said that if Sodom and Gomorrah has seen what Israel did,
They would have existed to that day.
The Father does not want anyone to perish
But that all come to a knowledge of His Christ.
The Glory of God manifested, sent the people of Israel
To John the Baptist in the desert;
The Glory of God manifested, caused three thousand people to come to Christ
In response to Peter's exhortation on The Day of Pentecost.
God the Father is the evangelist, we are simply His instruments.
The Glory of God manifested, produced every Revival God has sent.

Without A Vision The People Perish

Without a vision, without a revelation, no one can be saved.
This is a vision of God and His Christ, imparted by God and His Christ;
A vision of the Kingdom of God and His Glory;
A revelation of the forgiveness, mercy, grace and love extended by Christ Jesus.
Before any of us come to Christ Jesus
We have been wooed by the Father for a period of time.
This wooing develops a vision within us, a revelation within us.
This wooing is different as each of us is different.

The Season Of The Last Generation

YOUR KINGDOM COME ON EARTH AS IN HEAVEN

The Father's wooing is tailor made for each one of us.

Once saved, no one can maintain that saved condition
With out continuous revelation, without Christ living in us.
The apostle Paul said we are saved and being saved.
Christ becomes our teacher as He said He would.
When we are saved, the Father puts His law in our minds
And writes them upon our hearts.
This supernatural reality is to give us continuous vision, continuous revelation.
The gifts of the Spirit were given to give us continuous revelation.
Through these gifts God continuously renews our vision;
He makes things new every morning.

The Work Of The Devil Is To Eliminate Vision

Before a person is saved the devil does everything in his power
To keep them from seeing the Way, the Truth, and the LIFE.
At the same time, God is wooing every person,
Revealing His Christ and His Kingdom.
Often this leads to a crisis moment where the person must make a decision.

With Adam and Eve, the devil told them that there was something good
Outside of what God had told them, the knowledge of good and evil;
That with this knowledge they would be like God.
That they would not die as God has told them.
This was a lie, as they quickly found out.
They were innocent, pure, holy, undefiled and living in Paradise,
But they were able to be deceived.

Had they known what would happen they would have never believed the devil.
Nevertheless, God had made it plain
That they were not to eat of the Tree of the Knowledge of Good and Evil.
They had the choice to trust God or believe the serpent.
They made their choice, disobeyed God, and suffered the terrible consequences,
As did all of humanity that followed them.

The devil appealed to the pride of Adam and Eve;
He deceived them into thinking that they could be like God.
A totally irrational idea;
In fact the same idea that removed him from Heaven
And doomed him to eternal death.

The Focus Of The Work Of The Devil
Is To Eliminate The Vision Of God's Church

The whole world belongs to to the devil as the apostle John told us.

The Season Of The Last Generation

Deceiving the world presents no real challenge to him.
The Church is the only entity that stands in his way of total domination and control.
Once we are saved, the devil will do everything in his power
To eliminate the vision that God has given us and continues to give us.
God had given Adam and Eve everything in Paradise.
God has given us everything in Christ Jesus.
God is Love. He is only one who is good; He is everything that is good.
Outside of God there is nothing good!
Everything outside of God dies eternally.
As long as we maintain our God given vision,
That there is nothing good outside of Christ Jesus,
And that we have been given everything that is good in Him,
The devil will be powerless to deceive us.

God has made it possible for us to live in His Kingdom on earth as in Heaven.
We can live in the Secret Place of the Most High God;
We can live "in the Spirit," in His Anointing,
In His incomparable Presence and communion.
We can know joy unspeakable and full of glory.
It is true that we are still in a natural body,
But in every other respect we can live in His Kingdom,
The supernatural realm of God.
In this condition, the devil cannot touch us as the apostle John said.
As soon as we step out of this condition we are easy prey.

The Devil's Ancient Tools
1. <u>The lust of the flesh</u>: An insatiable sex drive that rules our lives; leading to sex outside of marriage, adultery, pornography, etc.
2. <u>The lust of the eyes</u>: Always wanting what we do not have; Envying what others have; Always wanting more, never satisfied.
3. <u>The pride of life</u>: Allowing what we have and what we can accomplish dominate our lives. Always wanting to out do the next person.

These are the devil's ancient tools to lead men and Christians astray;
The ancient tools he uses to destroy God's imparted vision.
His means of deceiving the Church of God are seen in Scripture.

The Deceived Church
1. <u>Having a form of faith in Christ but denying its power</u>: Saying that the gifts of the Spirit and the miracles of Christ are not for today. Such a Church renders itself blind. This is a Church without vision and naked. This is the Church that Christ Jesus encountered in His day. They diligently studied the Scriptures but could not recognize their Messiah. Their worship was only rules made up by men, and their hearts were far from Him.
2. <u>Claiming to belong to Christ but living like the devil</u>: This is the problem that

so many of the New testament letters address. These are people deceived and destined for hell unless they turn around and live for God.

3. <u>Having forsaken their first love</u>: Christ Jesus makes it very clear that maintaining our first love is critical.
4. <u>Thinking that they are alive but are actually dead</u>: By outward appearance this Church seems to be alive, but God does not look as man looks, He looks at the heart. If the heart is not right, it is not right with Him.
5. <u>The lukewarm Church, rich and in need of nothing</u>: This Church lacks first love, passion, and zeal for Christ. They have a fine church building, plenty of money, and everything that appeals to men but Christ Jesus spits such a Church out of His mouth.

All the Churches above have lost their vision
Through the deception of the devil.
The devil is very proficient at deceiving the Church of God.
This can be seen throughout the Old Testament,
It can be seen in the New Testament Letters,
It can be seen in the Seven Letters to the Seven Churches
In the Book of Revelation;
It can be seen from all of the last 2,000 years of Church history.

In fact, from the view of Scripture, and history,
There is far more deception in God's Church than there is faithfulness to Him.
Nevertheless, Christ Jesus said
That the gates of hell would not prevail against His Church,
Therefore, we know that this will be the case.

However, we also know that it was always a Remnant out of the larger body
That maintained their faithfulness to God.
We can fully expect this pattern to continue in our day, The Time Of The END.
There will be a Remnant who will maintain their God given "vision"
And not allow it to be dulled or destroyed by the deception of the devil.
In the time of Christ Jesus the Remnant included fishermen, tax collectors,
And a prostitutes; the most unlikely from a human point of view.

Living In His Presence Is The Ultimate Vision; In His Presence Time Is Suspended

In His Presence God reveals to us what He wants us to know;
What we need to know.
In HIs Presence time has no meaning, it does not exist
Because His Kingdom has come to earth as in Heaven;
Time does not exist in Heaven.
In His Presence you are made whole as you will be in Heaven
Unencumbered by the cares of this world.
In His Presence the cares of this world vanish;

The Season Of The Last Generation

You are lost in His love, mercy, and grace.
You have entered the Glory realm of God; you never want to leave.
It is as if you have died and gone to Heaven.
It is as if you have been born again, again.

When Christ Jesus returns, and we meet Him in the air, we shall be like Him,
Because we shall see Him as He is.
In the Glory realm of God you see Him as He is.
It is a foretaste of the permanent, supernatural reality that's coming.
You then become like Him, whole, complete as He is.
His Presence is intoxicating, as it was for the 120 on The Day of Pentecost;
It is full of fire, the all consuming fire of God,
Which eliminates everything unholy.
There is joy unspeakable and full of His Glory.
Christ causes some to laugh their way to wholeness.
This laughter can last for long periods of time,
As the God of Heaven gives you His supernatural joy, which is your strength.
This laughter is the medicine of Heaven, from God's own pharmacy.

Only children can enter this realm.
It is reserved for children.
The Glory realm of God cannot be intellectualized;
His ways are not the ways of man;
As high as the heavens are above the earth
So are the ways of God above the ways of man.
The Glory realm of God is reserved for children
Who are compelled by a child like faith and love,
To climb up into their Daddies lap, and love on Him as He loves on them.
You enter this realm as a child or you cannot enter.

In the Glory realm of God you may be in a large crowd
But it is as if you and Christ are completely alone.

There is no intimacy on earth like intimacy with Christ Jesus.
Every earthly experience pales by comparison.
It is a foretaste of Heaven.
This is what the Church of God needs to introduce to those who do not believe.
This is what brings people to Christ Jesus like no other.
God Himself is the evangelist, we are simply His instruments.

That is why David could say:
"One thing I ask, this is what I seek
That I may dwell in the house of the Lord, all the days of my life,
To gaze upon the beauty of the Lord and seek Him in His Temple."

The Season Of The Last Generation

YOUR KINGDOM COME ON EARTH AS IN HEAVEN

God had taken David into His Glory realm.
David knew what it was to live in the Secret Place of the Most High God.
To be covered with the feathers of God.

In the Glory realm of God the devil is driven out.
This can get exciting as devils are compelled to leave their hosts;
Not necessarily by prayer or any human intervention but by the Glory of God.
On the other hand there is an anointing the comes upon all present;
Some to minister and some to receive ministry.
Sometimes words are spoken, prophecy given, and sometimes no words at all.
Simply extending a hand toward someone can cause them to be slain in the Spirit.
Blowing on them can cause them to be slain in the Spirit.
The anointing of Christ Jesus is imparted to the ministers and His Glory manifested.
The Kingdom of God has come to earth as in Heaven.

David said that one day in the Lords' Presence was worth a thousand other days.
One meeting in the presence of the Lord is worth a thousand other meetings.
One word spoken by God is worth more than a thousand words from man.
God can give you, in a word or two, more profound meaning than a library.

Once you experience the Glory realm of God you are spoiled forever,
And that is exactly what God wants to accomplish in you.
Then you are willing to be crucified with Christ to this world and its miserable ways.
Then you will see this world as it is, a prideful pretense.

There was a sign along the interstate highway in Idaho where I was raised.
It said:

Are you lost? Don't worry about it, you're making good time.

That well describes the condition of the world and much of the Church.
The trouble is, the destination is hell.

For two thousand years the God of Heaven has been offering His Church
His new wine; His Kingdom on earth as in Heaven.
For two thousand years many have rejected it,
Saying that the old wine is better
Just as Christ Jesus said they would.
Men love a comfortable, repetitive, unsurprising religion that promises Heaven,
And demands little or nothing from them personally.
Whose worship is made up of the rules of men;
Men whose hearts are far from Him.

Nevertheless, there has always been a little band of children, a Remnant;
The original group included fishermen, tax collectors and a prostitutes,

The Season Of The Last Generation

Who were willing to take Christ Jesus at His Word.
Willing to drink the new wine.
Willing to be crucified to this world with Christ, to gain the Glory realm of God;
Willing to come to "know" the God of Heaven and His Christ.
Willing to pray Your Kingdom come, Your will be done, on earth as in Heaven
And mean it;
Willing to receive it when it came;
Many who are first will be last and the last will be first.

Think about it;
Virtually the whole religious hierarchy of Israel rejected Christ Jesus,
But a little band of children received Him.

Among those who will receive Him in our day will be the "Woman" of Revelation 12;
The Bride of Christ in this generation.
Who will mister in the fullness of Christ Jesus
For three and one-half years prior to The Great Tribulation;
Inviting all men to the Wedding Supper of the Lamb.
Just as John the Baptist did;
Just as Christ Jesus did.
Just as the first apostles and disciples did.
Just as God did with every Revival he sent up to this day.

Christ Jesus is sending His final Revival through the ministry of His Bride.
She will invite all men to the Wedding Supper of the Lamb.
All His children will receive their invitation; they will all be there;
Those who love Him with all their heart, soul, mind and strength.

Seek First The Kingdom Of God

Jesus tells His children to seek first, above all else, The Kingdom of God.
Where in His Presence, the things of this world grow dim.
His Kingdom, where Christ Jesus is lifted up to His rightful place;
Where He is seen as He is;
Lord of all, exalted King of the universe, Author of all creation, Author of Salvation,
Seated on the Throne of Heaven in all its incomparable Glory;
Friend and Lover.
From that position and revelation He draws all men to Himself;
All those destined to Heaven.

Seek first the Kingdom of God,
Where we become like Him because we see Him as He is.
Where there is righteous, peace and joy; where Love reigns.
Where His people are made whole in Him, complete in Him.
The Kingdom of God, where there is all provision for His people, lacking nothing.
The Kingdom of God, where His Almighty power is given to His people,

The Season Of The Last Generation

To accomplish His plan and His purposes.
The Kingdom of God where the River of God flows continually;
The River of delights.
Where the Living Water is served continually.
Where the people of God drink continually; are immersed continually,
In the atmosphere of His Glory.
Hallelujah!

The Season Of The Last Generation

THE KINGDOM OF GOD IS FOR CHILDREN ONLY!

***I tell you the truth, unless you change and become like children,
You will never enter the Kingdom of Heaven.***

*Therefore, whoever humbles himself like this child
Is the greatest in the Kingdom of Heaven.
And whoever welcomes a little child like this in my name welcomes me.
(Matthew 18:2-5)*

Jesus said:
*Let the little children come to me, and do not hinder them, for the Kingdom of
Heaven belongs to such as these. (Matthew 19:14)*

*How great is the love the Father has lavished on us,
That we should be called children of God! (1 John 3:1)*

**Every person is in fact, a child in comparison
To the all knowing, all seeing, all powerful, present everywhere,
Self-existent, God of creation.**

Children trust their fathers and are completely dependent upon them.
They love and idolize their fathers; they live to please them.
They rest in the assurance of their father's love.
They love to be in the presence of their father more than anything else;
They seek the approval of their father in all they do.
They allow their father to guide, direct and teach them.

This requirement of child likeness, as access to the Kingdom of God,
Has been an insurmountable barrier for many in every age.
It will be a insurmountable barrier for many in this day.
The Kingdom of God was made for children, by God, who is Love.
The River of God that runs through the middle of the City of God
Is a River of delights; it is delightful for children in the here and now
As well as the by and by.
A predominant characteristic of children is their desire to play.
A defining characteristic of a good father
Is his desire to play with and enjoy his children.

Our Heavenly Father is the Father of fathers.
He created the River of Delights specifically for His children.
Those who were privileged to experience the Renewal of the 90's
And it's continuation and other moves of God know this.
Laughter and shear happiness were characteristic of every Revival.

The Season Of The Last Generation

THE KINGDOM OF GOD IS FOR CHILDREN ONLY!

Yes, there was conviction of sin and the revelation of the holiness of God,
Repentance and forgiveness.
But along with this, and in equal measure,
Came the revelation of the goodness and love of God.

Christ Jesus said:
I praise you, Father, Lord of Heaven and earth,
Because you have hidden these things
(The reality of the Kingdom of God on earth as in Heaven)
From the wise and learned, and revealed them to little children.
Yes, Father, for this was your good pleasure. *(Matthew 11:25-26)*

God has said:
I will destroy the wisdom of the wise,
The intelligence of the intelligent I will frustrate. (Isaiah 29:14)

Christ Jesus said:
Wisdom (The Bride of Christ) *is proved right by her actions. (Matthew 11:19)*
Wisdom embraces Christ Jesus who is LIFE.

The Kingdom Of God Is Available To All Children Who Come To Christ Jesus In Faith

In the Gospels, Christ Jesus said: 'Repent for the Kingdom of heaven is near.'
(Matthew 4:17)
The Kingdom of God was near because Christ Jesus was near
And He embodied the Kingdom of God.
The "good news," is that the Kingdom of God is available
To any "child," who comes to Christ Jesus in faith with a gentle and humble heart.
On The Day of Pentecost the Kingdom of God came to earth as in Heaven;
That is Christ, the Holy Spirit came and inhabited His people
And there was a manifestation of that reality.

The Kingdom of God is the supernatural realm of God,
Created by the Father for His children.
It may be proclaimed by a man
But belief and confession can only be produce by God.
In salvation, it is God, touching the heart of a "child"
And reveling Himself to them.
Out of this revelation they are able to believe and make their confession of faith.
This revelation is initiate by God and completely supernatural;
The only part the "child" plays is to agree with the Father.

What does God say that the New Covenant is?
He tells us, that unlike the Old Covenant that remained in the natural,
In the New Covenant He places His law in our minds and writes it on our hearts;

The Season Of The Last Generation

THE KINGDOM OF GOD IS FOR CHILDREN ONLY!

This is a supernatural impartation done by God,
Creating a new supernatural being, a "born again" child of God.
Entering the Kingdom of God entails receiving a supernatural revelation from God,
That imparts belief, faith and Christ the Holy Spirit.
An impartation of His Kingdom on earth as in Heaven.
The Kingdom of God on earth is Christ in you the hope of glory, manifested;
That is the glory of Christ Jesus, manifested.

God's Kingdom Is The Realm Of His Spirit,
The Realm Of His Glory, Where He Rules And Reigns.

By definition any kingdom is where the king rules and reigns.
Christ Jesus teaches us to pray,
To ask the Father to bring His Kingdom to earth as in Heaven;
That His will would be done on earth as in Heaven.
That everything we do on earth as as followers of Christ
Would be as it is done in Heaven;
That everything that happens in and through His children becomes supernatural,
A manifestation of His glory.

Christ came to inhabit His children;
To rule and reign in them; to manifest Himself in and through them.

When Christ Jesus sent His disciples out,
He sent them out to preach this message:
"The Kingdom of Heaven is near."
Today, we preach that the Kingdom of God is "here."
He sent them out with His Glory, the Glory of His Kingdom.
He told them to heal the sick, raise the dead;
That what they were freely given (God's Kingdom Glory) they were to freely give.
This was before The Day of Pentecost;
It was an example of what was to happen, typically, after Pentecost;
It was an example of what did happen, typically, after Pentecost.

Where Christ Rules and Reigns
His Glory Will Be Made Manifest

The Scriptures teach that Christ Jesus worked with His disciples
And confirming His Word by the signs that accompanied it. (Mark 16:20)
The disciples testified to the Word of Christ, and Christ Jesus manifested His glory.
Wherever Christ rules and reigns this will be the case,
Where ever He rules and reigns,
His glory will be revealed in and through His children with signs and wonders.

THE KINGDOM OF GOD IS FOR CHILDREN ONLY!

Christ Can Only Rule And Reign
Where The Freedom He Brought, Rules and Reigns

It is for freedom that Christ has set us free.
Stand firm, then,
And do not let yourselves be burdened again by a yoke of slavery.
(Galatians 5:1)

Christ will only manifest his glory through "children"
In whom He rules and reigns;
Children who He has set free from sin
And the bondage of the rules and devices of men.

Christ can only be "lifted up" by "children" in whom He rules and reigns;
Children who have been set free by the Spirit of Christ;
Those who worship Him in Spirit and in Truth.
When He is "lifted up" by "children" who have been set free,
In who He rules and reigns,
Then He draws all men to Himself;
Then there is the continuous Revival he came to bring.
Christ will share His glory with no man.
He will not allow man to appropriate His glory.
That is exactly what the devil seeks to do.

Christ Jesus set us free from all forms of bondage.
In the New Covenant God eliminated any bondage of man
By eliminating any hierarchy of man
Between Himself and His children; He made His children all priests before Him.
He did this by His initiative; putting His law in their minds,
And writing them on the hearts of His children,
So that it would not be necessary for anyone to teach them to "know" Him,
Because they would all "know" Him from the least to the greatest.
God eliminated all intermediaries to "knowing" Him,
By the giving of the Holy Spirit, the anointing of the Anointed One.
God will have no one between each of His children and Himself.
Christ Jesus said we have One Teacher, the Christ.
(Jeremiah 31 and John 2)

Man made religion always creates a hierarchy that empowers a few.
People, in the natural, gravitate to a hierarchical religion,
Because it relieves them of their responsibility.
In the New Covenant each child is responsible for their relationship with their Father.
No one will have any excuse for not coming to "know" their God.
Each of us is "free" to "know" God the Father.
No one can keep this from us,

109

The Season Of The Last Generation

THE KINGDOM OF GOD IS FOR CHILDREN ONLY!

And God the Father continually pursues each one of us.

Christ Jesus said:
If you hold to my teaching, you are really my disciples.
Then you will know the truth and the truth will set you free. *(John 8:31-32)*

Freedom is beautiful;
It is Christ Jesus ruling and reigning in and through His children.
This is the only freedom that exists on the earth.

I tell you the truth, everyone who sins is a slave to sin.
Now a slave has no permanent place in the family,
But a son belongs to it forever.
So if the Son sets you free, you will be free indeed. (John 8:34-36)

The antithesis of freedom is man made religion.
It is specifically designed by the devil to bring bondage,
Because through bondage men gain control which is their objective,
Under the deception of the devil.
Remember, the devil masquerades as an angel of light
And man made religion is his primary tool.
Christianity is the primary target of the devil.
The freedom Christ Jesus brought is his only adversary.
The natural tendency of men is to lay burdens on people,
Whereas Christ Jesus is a burden lifter.

The apostle Paul said:
But thanks be to God that, though you used to be slaves to sin,
You wholeheartedly obeyed the form of teaching to which you were entrusted.
You have been set free from sin and have become slaves to righteousness.
(Romans 6:17-18)

Therefore, there is now no condemnation for those who are in Christ Jesus,
Because through Christ Jesus <u>the law of the Spirit of life</u> set me free
From the law of sin and death. (Romans 8:1-2)

I consider that our present sufferings are not worth comparing
With the glory that will be revealed in us.
The creation waits in eager expectation for the sons of God to be revealed.
For the creation was subjected to frustration, not by its own choice,
But by the will of the one who subjected it,
In hope that the creation itself will be liberated from its bondage to decay
And brought into the glorious freedom of the children of God.
(Romans 8:18-21)

The Season Of The Last Generation

THE KINGDOM OF GOD IS FOR CHILDREN ONLY!

Now the Lord is the Spirit,
And where the Spirit of the Lord is, there is freedom.
(2 Corinthians 3:17)

How do we know where the Spirit of the Lord is?
Where there is the freedom Christ died to bring.
It is sin for any one of us to allow anyone or any thing
To get between us and God the Father.
The Spirit of the Lord has set His children free from all forms of bondage,
Spiritual or man made.

The children of God have been set free by Christ in them
To be holy, free to live righteous, free to love without conditions;
Free to worship in Spirit and in Truth.

For if you live according to the sinful nature, you will die;
But if by the Spirit, you put do death the misdeeds of the body, you will live,
Because those who are led by the Spirit of God are sons of God.
For you did not receive a spirit that makes you a slave again to fear,
But you received the Spirit of sonship.
And by him we cry, 'Abba, Father.'
The Spirit himself testifies with our spirit that we are the children of God
And co-heirs—heirs with Christ,
If indeed we share in his sufferings in order that we may also share in his glory.
(Romans 8:13-17)

The "children" of God will not tolerate any form of bondage in their lives.
Bondage is repulsive to them; it opposes freedom.
All forms of bondage are anti-Christ.
Christ Jesus came to set His children free.
Where Christ Jesus rules and reigns His children are free.
The Bride of Christ has fought for freedom in every generation;
She, like her Savior, gave her life in every generation, to be free.
Father, give us resolve in Christ, to be free in this generation;
To allow Christ Jesus to rule and reign in and through us.

Children Express Their Freedom In Christ
By Their Praise And Worship To Christ

From the lips of children and infants you have ordained praise.
(Matthew 21:16)

The simplest way I have found to determine if there is freedom in a body
Is to observe their praise and worship to the Father.
If they are able to praise and worship as the Psalms instruct us,

111

THE KINGDOM OF GOD IS FOR CHILDREN ONLY!

Then, most often, there is freedom in that body.
If they do not, then there is usually bondage.
This is especially true of the leadership of a church.
If the leaders can express freedom themselves in praise and worship,
Then, they are usually able to be free and allow freedom.

The whole purpose of leadership in a church
Is to provide an atmosphere where Christ Jesus can rule and reign;
An atmosphere of freedom,
Where Christ Jesus is allowed to do what only He can do;
Manifest His glory, which is Revival, in every assembly.
Christ Jesus intended that His people be in continuous revival
From The Day of Pentecost till today;
That His people prophesy, dream dreams and have visions;
He is the Spirit of prophesy and all illumination for His children.
Christ Jesus provides "vision" for His children;
Without which they perish and with which they thrive.

Christ is the Spirit that produced the Psalms;
The Spirit that produced the Tabernacle of David and continuous praise and worship;
The Spirit that said in the last days he would rebuild the Tabernacle of David;
Zion where the fire of God resides; The New Jerusalem, which is God's furnace.
The Bride of Christ, in these last days, will manifest the glory of God.
She will lift Christ Jesus up, and He will draw all men to Himself.

WORSHIP GOD IN SPIRIT AND IN TRUTH

The Purpose of God In Creation
The purpose of God in creation was to obtain a Bride for His Son;
A Bride who of Her own free will would choose to marry His Son;
A Bride who would be commensurate with His Son in character and being;
A Bride who would love His Son as He loved His Son;
A Bride who would become ONE with His Son by the power of His Holy Spirit.
A Bride with whom His Son could enjoy intimate communion for eternity.
This purpose of God is the framework for all of Scriptural history.

In The New Covenant God Seeks Three Things
1. Those who will worship Him in Spirit and in Truth. (John 4:23)
2. Glory (John 8:50)
3. The lost (Luke 19:10)

It seems only logical that the Church of God would endeavor
To give to their God what He seeks when it is possible for them to do so.
When the people of God worship Him in Spirit and in Truth;
That is in and through Christ in them,
He releases His manifest, tangible Presence and Glory;
This brings about a God consciousness in believers and unbelievers,
And all know assuredly that Christ Jesus was sent as their Lord and Savior.
Today, Christ Jesus is seeking those who will worship Him in Spirit and in Truth,
Who love Him with all their heart, soul, mind and strength
So that the whole world will know that Christ Jesus was sent by God the Father.

True Worshipers
Jesus said to the woman at the well:
Believe me woman, a time is coming
When you will worship the Father neither on this mountain nor in Jerusalem.
You Samaritans worship what you do not know;
We worship what we do know;
For salvation is from the Jews.
Yet a time is coming and has now come
When the true worshipers will worship the Father in Spirit and in Truth,
For they are the kind of worshipers the Father seeks.
God is Spirit, and his worshipers must worship in Spirit and in Truth. (John 4:21-24)

When the people of God worship in Spirit and in Truth,
They are worshiping in and through Christ, who is the Spirit, who is the Truth;
Then God manifests Himself.

The Season Of The Last Generation

It is not a specific place; it can be any place where this occurs.
When the people of God worship Him in His Spirit and in His Truth;
Through Christ in them; having been born again of His Spirit;
Then He reveals His manifest Presence and Glory.
The people of God must worship in Spirit and in Truth.

Your Kingdom Come On Earth As In Heaven
The primary objective of God on earth is to raise up a Bride for His Son;
A Bride who will become ONE with Him by the power of His Spirit in Her.
Then His Kingdom comes to earth as in Heaven.
Then Christ Jesus rules and reigns on earth as in Heaven
The Bride of Christ seeks the Kingdom of God above all else
As Christ Jesus admonished;
He placed it within in her, the Holy Spirit in her, Christ in her,
But it only has value as it is made manifest and demonstrated,
As can be seen from the Book of Acts.

The Lord taught His disciples how to pray,
Your Kingdom come to earth as in Heaven.
From Scripture we can see that in Heaven there is continuous worship.
The Bride of Christ brings the Kingdom of God to earth as in Heaven
When the people of God worship God as it is done in Heaven.
This is what occurred in The Tabernacle of David and is our example.
The Psalms, many of which were born out of the Tabernacle of David,
Are our teacher.
When the Kingdom of God comes to earth as in Heaven,
The devil is excluded, his work destroyed.
The devil has no access to the Kingdom of God;
When the Kingdom of God comes to earth as in Heaven
The Presence and Glory of God are manifested unhindered
By the evil, demonic principalities and powers in the heavenly realms.

Seek First The Kingdom Of God
Christ Jesus taught His disciples to seek first and above all else The Kingdom of God.
The Kingdom where Christ Jesus rules and reigns;
Where His Presence is manifested; where the devil is shut out.
Access to His Presence, to His Kingdom, is worship in Spirit and in Truth.

Meetings Consecrated By His Glory
The primary purpose in Christians gathering together
Should be the same as it was in the days of Moses
And the original Tent of Meeting, the "prototype" for the Church today;
That is to meet with God, that He might speak to us.
When we meet for this primary purpose,
Then God will consecrate the meeting by His Glory;

114

The Season Of The Last Generation

Then He will dwell in our midst;
Then we will know that He is our God who brought us out of Egypt;
Then we are differentiated from all the other peoples of the earth;
Then the peoples of the earth will know where to come to meet with God;
In the midst of the people of God; in the midst of His Glory.

For generations to come this burnt offering (worship) *is to be made regularly*
At the entrance to the Tent of Meeting before the Lord.
There I will meet you and speak to you;
There I will meet with the Israelites,
And the place will be consecrated by my glory.

So I will consecrate the Tent of Meeting and the altar and will consecrate
Aaron and his sons to serve me as priests.
Then I will dwell among the Israelites and be their God.
They will know that I am the Lord their God, who brought them out of Egypt
So that I might dwell among them.
I am the Lord their God. *(Exodus 29:42-46)*

It is the desire of God to meet and speak with us,
To consecrate our meetings with His glory;
Then His Kingdom comes to earth as in Heaven;
Then it is clear who belongs to God and who does not;
Then the people He calls by His Spirit know where to come to meet Him;
Then He adds people to His Bride according to His will.
The whole purpose of "Church" or assembling together
Is so that God can meet with us, speak to us and add to us.

What does A New Covenant Assembly Look Like?

The apostle Paul describes this:
When you come together, everyone has a hymn, or a word of instruction,
A revelation, a tongue or an interpretation.
All of these must be done for the strengthening of the church.
If anyone speaks in a tongue, two—or at the most three—should speak,
One at a time, and someone must interpret.
If there is no interpreter, the speaker should keep quiet in the church
And speak to himself and God.

Two or three prophets should speak,
And the others should weigh carefully what is said.
And if a revelation comes to someone who is sitting down,
The first speaker should stop.
For you can all prophesy in turn
So that everyone may be instructed and encouraged.
The spirits of prophets are subject to the control of prophets.

For God is not a God of disorder but of peace. (1 Corinthians 14:26-33)

The House of Praise Was At The Entrance To The Tabernacle
In the layout of the tribes of Israel around the Tabernacle of Moses,
The House of Praise, the Tribe of Judah,
Was positioned at the entrance to the Tabernacle.
Even the tents of Moses and Aaron were outside of the Tribe of Judah.
This was God speaking eloquently about the importance of praise
In the Old Covenant and its fulfillment in the New Covenant,
Praise is central to worship.
Access through His gates and into His courts is praise.
Access to the Holy Place and the Holy of Holies is intimate worship,
From a consecrated people.

When We Meet With God Our Face Will Shine
When Moses met with God his face shone with the Glory of God.
God wants the face of His Church to shine with the Glory of God.
When Steven testified for God his face shone with the Glory of God;
He looked like and angel;
When you stand in the Presence of God your face will shine with His Glory.

When You Meet With God You Will Be Forever Changed
Abraham heard from God and was willing to leave his homeland
And go to a place he never knew.
God changed Abraham's name and his destiny with a covenant.
Jacob wrestled with God and had his name and his nature changed;
God gave him a permanent physical mark of that meeting.
Moses met God and was commissioned with a task and destiny;
To deliver Israel from Egypt.
He was changed from shepherd to deliverer.
David met God and had only one desire in life; to be in His Presence;
He was changed from shepherd to king, psalmist and prophet.
On the Day of Pentecost, the Church met God and were intoxicated with His Glory,
Spoke in languages they did not know,
And went on to change the world through Christ in them.
When God met you, you were changed from being dead, to being alive in Christ.
You can now do exceedingly and abundantly above what you can think or ask
Because of the power of Christ in you.

Access To The Presence Of God:
The Mercy Seat Which Was Over The Ark Of His Presence
In The Most Holy Place
The Mercy Seat provides our only approach to God.

The Season Of The Last Generation

Because it has been sprinkled with the blood of Christ,
The same blood we have applied to our lives having received Christ by faith.
The Mercy Seat, sprinkled with the blood of Christ Jesus
Allows God to meet with us and speak to us.

Access To The Most Holy Place
The sacrifice of praise and thanksgiving allows us to enter the courts of God,
And place our offering on the Brazen Altar,
But the Mercy Seat, where God speaks to us, is in the Most Holy Place.
To get to the Most Holy Place we must enter the Holy Place.
To enter the Holy Place we must be a priest, consecrated to God,
Washed, anointed, clothed with Christ and sprinkled and applied with His blood.
To enter the Most Holy Place we must then offer sacred incense, acceptable to God;
True worship from our hearts that touches His heart;
Worship in Spirit and in Truth.

We Know That Our Worship Has Touched The Heart Of God When He Speaks To Us And Reveals His Presence And Glory
That is God's way of acknowledging that our worship has reached Him,
And is acceptable to Him.
God lives in the praises of His people;
We become ONE with Him as we praise and then worship Him;
We are transformed by the words of our mouth, coming from our hearts;
We may begin in the natural but we then allow Christ in us to take over,
Which allows us to enter the supernatural, the realm of the Spirit of God;
The Gory realm of God.

In the Book of Revelation the apostle John said
That he was "in the Spirit" on the Lord's day.
In this condition, Christ Jesus was able to speak to him
And give him a great revelation; the Book of Revelation.
Praise and Worship enables us to get "in the Spirit;"
When we are "in the Spirit" God can speak to us as He desires.
To hear from God we must get "in the Spirit."
All those "in the Spirit" are ONE with God and each other.

When we are in the Glory realm of God
He manifests His Presence and Glory;
He speaks to us, He communes with us, He loves on us and we love on Him.
In the atmosphere of His Presence and Glory sinners come to Christ Jesus;
Then the sick are healed and the dead are raised.
All things are possible and come to pass in the Glory realm of God.
In the atmosphere of the Presence and Glory of God the devil is driven out.

WORSHIP GOD IN SPIRIT AND IN TRUTH

We must not satisfy ourselves with glimpses of His Presence and Glory.
God wants to immerse us in His Glory continually;
He wants us to live in "The Secret Place of the Most High God;"
He wants His Kingdom to come to earth as in Heaven and reside there, continually.
His objective is that we become ONE with Him and live in His Presence.
We need to press into worship
Until we are immersed in His Presence and Glory.

True worship lifts Christ up and allows God to manifest His Presence;
Then He draws all men to Himself;
This is New Covenant evangelism and the Glory He is seeking;
God is glorified when His people worship Him in Spirit and in Truth;
God is glorified when people accept His Christ as their Lord and Savior
Every Christian can participate in this most glorious enterprise;
No one is excluded; nothing is more important.

The Bride Of Christ Will Join With David In Asking But One Thing

One thing I ask, *this is what I seek*
That I may dwell in the house of the Lord
All the days of my life
To gaze upon the beauty of the Lord
And seek Him in His temple. (Psalm 27:4)

As God Seeks those who will worship Him in Spirit and in Truth,
The Bride of Christ seeks to worship Him who is the Spirit and the Truth;
To gaze upon the beauty of the Lord
And they become ONE; the Glory of Christ Jesus is manifested;
Sinners come to Christ Jesus as the incense of Praise and Worship
Covers the Mercy Seat and access to the Presence is opened.

True Worship To The Living God Comes From The Heart
The Tabernacle of David, Zion, Exemplified This Worship

Unless the Lord builds the house, its builders labor in vain. (Psalm 127:1)

The Lord is the architect and builder of Zion; David was an instrument.
The house of God is built with living stones,
Those filled with Christ, who is LIFE.
The fire of God is in Zion, his furnace in Jerusalem (His Church). (Isaiah 31:9)
God infuses The Bride of Christ with His fire.
Her love for Him is as strong as death and burns like a blazing fire.
The House of God is built with Living Stones on Fire.

The Season Of The Last Generation

True worship is born out of the fire of God.
And comes from a consecrated heart.
It is based on an understanding of who is being worshiped.
You have to "know" God to be able to worship Him as God.
You have to "know" God to worship in His Spirit and in His Truth.
King David was a man after God's own heart.
David sought <u>one thing</u> above all else: the heart of God.
King David sought the heart of God and found Him as the Psalms attest.

David knew where he came from; watching over the sheep.
He knew that God had brought him from death to LIFE,
From shepherd to king;
That his LIFE was found in the Presence of God by the Holy Spirit within him.

God showed David, Gad and Nathan what true worship was to consist of,
And David built his Tabernacle and operated in it accordingly.
It was not elaborate, only a simple tent.
The Tabernacle of David exemplified the praise and worship that God seeks.
Because there He was worshiped in Spirit and in Truth.
That is why it is called Zion, the City of God, where the fire of God resides,
Foreshadowing the New Jerusalem that was to come;
The final and eternal City of the Living God, The Bride of Christ.

God revealed Himself to David and all Israel through His manifest Presence;
God supernaturally "kept" and prospered Israel for 36 years during David's reign.
The Tabernacle of David, was the vehicle that brought this about.
It is the prototype of God's desire for His Church today.
God was enthroned on the praises that emanated from the Tabernacle of David.
He desires to be enthroned on the praise of His Church today.
That is what it means to "lift Jesus up."
He is lifted up when we enthrone Him on our praise and worship.
He then draws all men to Himself; New Covenant evangelism.
God will "keep" and prosper His Church today
When we enthrone Him in our praise and worship from our hearts;
Then, He will live in the praises of His people and manifest his Presence;
Pushing back the evil, demonic authorities and powers in the heavenly realms
Giving the people of God victory wherever they are;
Creating the "open Heaven" so often spoken of, the Glory realm of God.

The Tabernacle of David was and is called Zion,
God's "Holy Hill," the City of God,
The Israel of God, the Church of God, the Bride of Christ, the Heart of God;
Zion comprises a people, abandoned to God, who have laid down their lives,
And become ONE with Christ Jesus and the Father,
In accordance with the prayer of Christ Jesus in John 17;

The Season Of The Last Generation

A people in complete unity; ONE with God, by the power of the Spirit of God.

In the last days, in our day, God promises to rebuild David's fallen tent:
After this I will return and rebuild David's fallen tent.
Its ruins I will rebuild, and I will restore it,
That the remnant of men may seek the Lord,
And all the Gentiles who bear my name, says the Lord, who does these things'
That have been known for ages. (Acts 15:16-18)

The Tabernacle of David will be rebuilt that the remnant of men may seek the Lord
In the last days.

Worship In Spirit And In Truth Eliminates the Veil
The Ark of the Covenant in The Tabernacle of David was not behind a veil.
There was no need for this because there was continuous worship
The worshipers were ONE with their God and there was no need for separation.
Their worship was a sweet smelling incense offered up to God
That covered the Mercy Seat.
Worshiping in Spirit and in Truth protected them from the awesome holiness of God;
The same holiness that killed Uzzah when he irreverently touched the ark.

King David understood this and set up The Tabernacle of David to this end.
The Tabernacle worshipers offered God continual worship, 24 hours a day.
The Tabernacle of David is the type worship
That God intended that we possess in the New Covenant;
That we continually worship God in Spirit and in Truth.
That we live continually in His Presence, continually in His Glory.

On The Day Of Pentecost, And Thereafter,
God Poured Out His Spirit On All Flesh
To enable us to get "in the Spirit" and out of the flesh,
So that He might meet with us individually and corporately and speak to us.
The apostle Peter declare about this day:

In the last days (the final two thousand years of "Time")
I will pour out my Spirit on all people.
Your sons and daughters will prophesy
(That is hear from God and speak that received to His people),
Your young men will see visions, your old men dream dreams.
Even on my servants, both men and women,
I will pour out my Spirit in those days, and they will prophesy. (Acts 2:17-18)

The Day of Pentecost was the beginning of a Revival that was to never end,
And it continues to this day in the hearts of those called by God.

The Season Of The Last Generation

Christ Jesus Provides Vision For His Church

In the Old Covenant this was the pillar of cloud by day
And the pillar of fire by night.
They were baptized into Moses and the sea;
The drank from the Rock which was Christ.

In the New Covenant we are led by Christ in us;
Without "vision" or "revelation" the Church of God perishes.
Prophesy, dreams and visions give the Body of Christ the "vision" they need
So that they will not perish;
Allowing the "charismatic" Christ in them to provide all necessary illumination.
The Scriptures teach that Christ Jesus is the Spirit of prophesy;
Christ in His Body provides "vision" and "revelation;"
Christ leads His Body into all Truth and tells them what is yet to come.
We eat the Bread from Heaven, Christ, the Bread of LIFE;
We drink the Water of LIFE, from Christ in us;
We live by every word that proceeds from the mouth of God.

Pentecost Began A Never Ending Revival

The Day of Pentecost ignited a never ending Revival;
The Father imparted His Holy Spirit to indwell His saints;
He baptized (immersed) His saints in the Holy Spirit and Fire.
They received power when this happened;
Power to live for Christ and power to do the works of Christ.
Christ Jesus said He came to bring a fire;
This fire was ignited on The Day of Pentecost
And has been burning in every generation since.
The only people who can worship in Spirit and in Truth
Are those who have received their personal Day of Pentecost.
Christ Jesus is "The Charismatic" and the "Inventor of Pentecost."
On the Day of Pentecost He gave birth to a "Charismatic people;"
He, reproduced Himself in His people, Christ in them their hope of Glory,
As the Book of acts clearly demonstrates.
Christianity, is Christ reproducing Himself in His people.

Revivals Are Times And Meetings Consecrated By God's Glory

God consecrated the meetings of John Westley and George Whitfield
With His Glory as they broke from the Church of England
To preach the Gospel to the common people in the open fields of the countryside.
God consecrated the meetings of the First Great Awakening in America.
For approximately ten years God reawakened America to the reality of His Christ;
Falling upon whole communities and regions,

The Season Of The Last Generation

WORSHIP GOD IN SPIRIT AND IN TRUTH

Using Johnathan Edwards as one of the instruments of His Glory.
God consecrated the meetings of the Second Great Awakening for many years,
As He reawakened America to the reality of His Christ;
Using Charles Finney as one of the instruments of His Glory.
God consecrated the meetings of Maria Etter with His Glory,
Falling on whole communities and regions, healing the worst diseases and afflictions.
God brought America and the world to the Azusa Street Mission
And William Seymour in a great move of the Spirit of God, revealing His Glory.
God poured out His Spirit on mainline churches,
In the Charismatic Renewal, revealing His Glory.
God brought the world to Toronto, Canada to experience His manifest Presence;
Consecrating the meetings with His Glory.
God brought people from far and wide to Brownsville, Florida
To give their lives to Christ and to be baptized.

These are but a few examples of the meetings and Revivals
God has visited upon His Church, consecrated by His Glory.
The out working of each of these "Revivals" continues to this day,
And all of them find their origin in The Day of Pentecost.

Give Me No Rest And Give Yourselves No Rest
Until Zion Is Made The Praise Of The Earth
God says to every Christian: *"Give yourselves no rest,*
And give Me no rest, until Zion is made the praise of the earth." (Isaiah 62)
Zion will be made the praise of the earth by the power of the Spirit of God
In those who worship God in Spirit and in Truth, in the here and now,
And bring the Kingdom of God to earth as in heaven.

The Old Covenant And It's Ark
The Ark of the Covenant was first made to reside in The Tabernacle of Moses.
It contained the Ten Commandments on tablets of stone,
The container of manna and Aaron's rod that budded.
The Ark stood behind the veil in the Holy of Holies.
Daily, the high priest burned incense before the veil which was before the Ark.
This incense was symbolic of the worship in The Tabernacle of David.
The worship in The Tabernacle of David
Allowed God to have the Ark of His Presence, unveiled;
It allowed God to continually release His Glory and Presence.
In the Tabernacle of Moses, once a year, the high priest went behind the veil,
Without his priestly garments, barefoot,
To sprinkle the Mercy Seat with blood, to atone for the sins of the nation.
He went before the Mercy Seat, vulnerable, risking his life.
Just as with the high priest, in worship, we come before the Mercy Seat of Christ.
When we worship in Spirit and in Truth our worship is acceptable to God.

The Season Of The Last Generation

We are testifying that we filled with Christ, and living in the New Covenant
Purchased by the blood of Christ Jesus
That He, Himself, sprinkled on the Mercy Seat in Heaven for us.
Our very lives have been purchased by the blood of Christ Jesus.
Christ Jesus found us dead and has given us LIFE.
Our worship is our response to that reality.

The New Covenant Ark

In the New Covenant God, takes His law out of the box, the Ark,
And puts it in the minds and writes it on the hearts of His people,
Immersing them in the Holy Spirit; saturating them in the Holy Spirit.
Again and again, forever;
Continually satisfying their never ending thirst for His Living Water.
Christ Jesus is the Bread of Heaven for those who eat of Him, continually.
Christ Jesus is the rod that budded, the "Branch" who blooms His Church.
In the New Covenant worship in Spirit and Truth removes the veil to His Presence,
And allows God to release His Presence and Glory.
When we fail to worship Him in Spirit and in Truth
He cannot release His Presence and His Glory, otherwise we would die;
If we are not in a consecrated state before Him,
And His Presence is released, we would die.
God is God of the Old and new Covenants, He never changes.
His Presence is sacred and awesome;
No unsanctified, unconsecrated person can stand in His Presence.
At the Battle of Armageddon,
Christ Jesus defeats Satan with the Glory of His appearing; His Presence,
And the word of His mouth.

In the New Covenant the Church,
The Bride of Christ, contains His Glory; Christ in us,
But this Glory is only manifested
When she is in a sanctified, consecrated state before Him.
Jesus declared that He had given the people of God His Glory in John 17;
That is for a remnant, and it has always been a remnant, throughout the ages.
It will be true for The Bride of Christ in The Time Of The END.
It will be true for those who love God
With all their hearts, soul, mind and strength;
Who have a passion for the New Covenant and the "new wine" it consists of.
Many will say the "old wine" is better
As Christ Jesus said of the Jewish religion of His day;
Many prefer a religion that has "form,"
And demands virtually nothing except rote tradition and rules made by men.
Such religion is a useless pretense, and does not have the power to save anyone.
Such religion always resists the Holy Spirit;
And hates those who are filled with the Spirit and operate in the Spirit,

The Season Of The Last Generation

As Stephen, the first martyr of the Church testified, before he was stoned to death.

His Presence Makes A Way Where There Is No Way
The Presence of God parted the Red Sea
Allowing the Israelites to escape their enemies.
The Ark of His Presence parted the Jordan River
And allowed the Israelites to cross over into the Promised Land.
God's Presence caused the walls of Jericho to fall down.
His Presence will take The Bride of Christ into the desert on the wings of an eagle,
Just as the children of Israel were taken into the desert on the wings of an eagle.
His Presence makes a way where there is no way.
Worship in Spirit and in Truth brings His Presence.

Christ Jesus, Lifted Up, Draws All Men To Himself
When Christ Jesus is lifted up in true worship,
When He is enthroned on the praises of His people,
He draws all men to Himself;
This is the purpose of worship and the plan of salvation;
That men get saved and live saved,
In an environment of continual worship, on earth as in Heaven.
God intended that every Christian be a full participant
In this glorious enterprise.

An Old covenant example of this involved Moses a "type" of Christ:
The Amalekites came and attacked the Israelites at Rephidim.
Moses said to Joshua, 'Choose some of our men and go out to fight the Amalekites.
Tomorrow I will stand on top of the hill with the staff of God in my hands.'
So Joshua fought the Amalekites as Moses had ordered,
And Moses, Aaron and Hur went to the top of the hill.
As long as Moses held up his hands, the Israelites were winning,
But whenever he lowered his hands, the Amalekites were winning.
When Moses' hands grew tired,
They took a stone and put it under him and he sat on it.
Aaron and Hur held his hands up—one on one side, one on the other--
So that his hands remained steady till sunset.
So Joshua overcame the Amalekite army with the sword.(Exodus 17:8-13)

Moses built an altar and called it The Lord is my Banner.
He said, 'For hands were lifted up to the throne of the Lord.
The Lord will be at war against the Amalekites form generation to generation.'

The power of God is released on our behalf
When we lift up our hands to the throne of the Lord in the New Covenant,
And we gain victory over our enemies.

The Season Of The Last Generation

WORSHIP GOD IN SPIRIT AND IN TRUTH

Lifting hands to the Lord is worship.
It is also instructive that Moses could not do it on his own, he needed help.
In the New Covenant as we lift each other up the power of God is released.
The more of us lifting up Christ Jesus and each other the more power is released.
The Lord is our Banner and our hands uplifted to Him become His banner,
Before which His enemies and ours are defeated.

True Worship Is Irresistible To All Who Hear God's Call

God is continually speaking to, calling, every living person.
True worship is irresistible to those who hear the call of God.
When the Body of Christ worships God in His Spirit and in His Truth,
The manifest Presence of God comes.
His Presence clears the Church and the geographical area
Of the domineering, demonic spirits that otherwise rule;
Unsaved people are released from their control and bondage,
And become free to choose Christ Jesus as their Lord and Savior;
Free to be immersed, baptized in His Spirit and set free.
True worship, sets everyone free
Free to worship their God in Spirit and in Truth.
As true worship progresses,
Whole regions and nations can be brought to Christ Jesus.
This is what is called "Revival"
That has occurred many times since the resurrection of Christ Jesus.
The Day of Pentecost was a "Revival" that was to never end and it never did end.
And all subsequent Revivals will have the characteristics of The Day of Pentecost,
Because all Revivals emanate from The Day of Pentecost and
Because Christ Jesus is "The Charismatic," "The Inventor of Pentecost."

Worship In Spirit And In Truth
Causes The River Of God To Flow
And The River Of God Brings The Water Of LIFE

Christ Jesus came to give us LIFE in His Spirit.
He is LIFE, the eternal, unchangeable LIFE; the Self-Existent LIFE.
The essence of God is found in His River of LIFE.
The River of God runs through the middle of the City of God, Zion,
The Bride of Christ, the Church of God, the Israel of God.
Bringing continual LIFE to it.
The River of LIFE contains the Water of LIFE that Christ Jesus came to bring.
Christ Jesus said that those who were thirsty could come to Him
And He would give them streams of Living Water
That would flow from their innermost being.
This flow is initiated by the immersion or baptism in the Holy Spirit
Just as the 120 received on The Day of Pentecost, and all those thereafter.
We find LIFE in His Spirit when we allow Christ, the River of LIFE

The Season Of The Last Generation

To flow in and through us.
Worship in Spirit and in Truth is produced by Christ in us.
He is the Spirit and He is the Truth; He is the Water of LIFE.
We worship in Spirit and in Truth,
When we allow the Spirit to worship in and through us.
Then we experience the freedom and victory Christ Jesus came to bring;
Then He releases His Presence and Glory.
The joy we find in this reality is our strength.

To Those Who Have, Even More Will Be Given
Wherever we are in God He always has more for us, forever.
Our infinite God has an infinite amount to give.
We all must have something, to be given more.
Christ Jesus begins by giving us a measure of faith in Him.
We then make a confession of that faith.
As we press into that faith He gives us more faith;
He immerses us, baptizes us in His Holy Spirit.
This is just the beginning of what can be a never ending increase.
There is an infinite supply of the Water of LIFE in the River of LIFE.
To those who have, even more will be given, forever.

When we worship God in Spirit and in Truth,
We are drinking from the River of LIFE;
The more we drink the more LIFE we have,
The more LIFE we have the more He can give to us.
Having more is only determined by how much we want.

For Christ Jesus, His zeal for God consumed Him.
He had food to eat that no one knew of, that came directly from His Father.
For the apostle Paul,
God did exceedingly and abundantly above what he could think or ask.
No eye has seen, no ear has heard what God has prepared for those who love Him
But He has revealed it to us by His Spirit,
And the Spirit searches all things even the deep things of God.
David asked for one thing: More of God
David knew that one day in the Presence of God was worth a thousand other days.
One meeting in the Presence of God is worth a thousand other meetings.
One word spoken by God is worth a thousand words spoken by man;
One "quickened" word from God is priceless.

Jesus said: *To Him who is thirsty*
I will give to drink without cost from the spring of the water of life.
He who overcomes will inherit **all this,**
And I will be his God and he will be my son. (Revelation 21:6-7)
All this is the infinite provision of the Spirit of the Living God.

The Season Of The Last Generation

Every Work For God Must Spring From True Worship

When the people of God submit themselves to Christ Jesus
And worship their God in Spirit and in Truth
God manifests His Glory and accomplishes His plan and purposes.
Every work for God must spring from true worship,
And be infused with His Glory;
Then its yoke is easy and its burden light.
The people asked Christ Jesus what work God required of them.
He told them the work required of them was to believe in the One God sent.
If we believe, we have faith, if we have faith, we seek the face of God.
If we seek the face of God, He reveals Himself to us;
He reveals His Glory, His manifest Presence.
Then all things are possible;
Then His plan and purposes are accomplished.

True Worship Comes From An Altar Of Uncut Stones

True worship is accomplished in us, through Christ;
We do not create it, He creates it in us.
True worship will create an altar to God untouched by the hands of man.
Often, we begin in the natural, but must allow Christ to take over.
If He does not take over, it is not true worship in Spirit and in Truth.

Elisha needed a word from God.
He called for the harpist
To help him get out of the natural into the supernatural.
Once in the supernatural, he received the word from God he needed.
The key to worshiping in Spirit and in Truth is to allow God to take over.
To loose our self-consciousness and become God conscious;
To get "in the Spirit;" to abandon ourselves to God.
Skill can be helpful or a hindrance depending ones willingness to let go.
If we hold too tightly to the "form" we will miss the substance.
As has been said, We must let go and let God.

Manifestations of uncut stone, altar worship include:
Prophetic words, words of knowledge, words of wisdom
A new song, born out of the Spirit of Christ in us;
Singing in the Spirit; dancing in the Spirit; marching in the Spirit;
Running in the Spirit; Shouting in the Spirit;
Impromptu instrumentals, involving one or more instruments, etc.
These are all expressions of the freedom Christ died to bring to His people;
Expressions of worshiping in Spirit and in Truth.

Extravagant Worship Releases The Fragrance Of Christ

The sinful woman who came to anoint Christ Jesus is an example of true worship.
Profound gratitude compelled her to show Him extravagant worship
For the extravagant act of forgiveness and salvation He had extended to her.
She willingly expended a years wages to anoint Him with a precious perfume;
She gave to Christ Jesus all that she had to give,
Just as Christ Jesus gives us all He has to give, which is everything worth having.
This woman sets a standard for the Body of Christ.
It is a high bar.
What is LIFE worth? LIFE comprising all that Christ gives to us.
Why do we worship? Because He loves us and gives us all He has to give,
Which is wonderful, beyond calculation; holding nothing back!
This woman's act of worship released a fragrance.
As we worship the fragrance of Christ is released,
And there are no limits to the extent of its influence.

We Do Not Struggle Against Flesh And Blood (Ephesians 6)

Our struggle is against the devil's schemes;
Against rulers, authorities and powers in this dark world
And against the spiritual forces of evil in heavenly realms.
Only the Lord, Christ in us, is able to bring victory against these adversaries.
These were the real enemies that came against King Jehoshaphat and Israel,
And through the praise of His people, the Lord brought them victory.
The devil must stand down, stand back and depart,
When the people of God praise their God.

Put On The Full Armor Of God (Ephesians 6)

What is our part in the battle?
To be strong in the Lord and in His mighty power;
To put on all that the Lord has given us, the full armor of God:
  • The belt of Truth
  • The breastplate of righteousness
  • Readiness to proclaim the good news
  • The shield of faith
  • The helmet of salvation
  • The sword of the Spirit
Then we are to stand in this armor and pray in the Spirit;
Worship in Spirit and in Truth.

The Battle Belongs To The Lord

This principle is taught to us in 2 Chronicles 20.
King Jehoshaphat is told that a vast army was coming against him.
He was alarmed and determined to inquire of the Lord as to what to do.

128

The Season Of The Last Generation

He proclaimed a fast for the nation;
The whole nation came to Jerusalem and the temple and stood before the Lord.
King Jehoshaphat prayed to the Lord.
He declared that the Lord is the God of heaven
Who rules over all the kingdoms of the earth;
Who promised that if His people would stand in His Presence and cry out to Him,
He would hear and save His people.
King Jehoshaphat said, we do not know what do do, but our eyes are fixed upon You.

Then the Spirit of the Lord came upon one of the Levities,
And he prophesied, do not be discouraged
Because the battle belongs to the Lord.
The Lord instructed the people to march down against the enemy,
Telling them that they would not have to fight.
Then some of the Levities stood and praised the Lord, the God of Israel
With a very loud voice.

The next morning King Jehoshaphat stood before the people and told them
To have faith in the Lord and His prophets and they would be successful.
After consulting with the people, he appointed men to sing to the Lord
And to praise Him for the splendor of his holiness;
They went out at the head of the army, singing:
"Give thanks to the Lord, for His love endures forever."
As they began to sing and praise, the Lord set ambushes against the enemy,
And they were completely defeated.
The Lord rose up on the praises of His people and destroyed the enemy.
The Lord will rise up on our praises today and give us victory.

The Kingdom Of God Advances Forcefully
And Forceful Men Lay Hold Of It
From the days of John the Baptist until now, the kingdom of heaven
Has been forcefully advancing, and forceful men lay hold of it. (Matthew 11:12)

Jehoash king of Israel came to see Elisha who was dying:
Elisha said, 'Get a bow and some arrows,' and he did so .
'Take the bow in your hands,' he said to the king of Israel.
When he had taken it, Elisha put his hands on the king's hands.

'Open the east window,' he said, and he opened it.
'Shoot!' Elisha said, and he shot.
'The Lord's arrow of victory, the arrow of victory over Aram!'
Elisha declared. 'You will completely destroy the Arameans at Aphek.'

Then he said, 'Take the arrows,' and the king took them .
Elisha told him, 'Strike the ground,'

He struck it three times and stopped.
The man of God was angry with him and said,
'You should have struck the ground five or six times,
Then you would have defeated Aram and completely destroyed it.
But now you will defeat it only three times.'

What Elisha told king Jehoash is a worship principle.
If we want victory in our worship we must persist into His Presence
And through His Presence to complete victory.
We must not stop before we have complete victory.
We must stop only when the Spirit releases us to stop.

God desires that we achieve victory over our enemy in our worship;
He has provide the means for us to do this by His Presence.
However, if we do not press in forcefully, until our enemy is destroyed,
We will have only a partial victory at best.
We cannot content ourselves with partial victories;
Our enemy does not.
He wants to see us completely destroyed and eternally dead.
This is similar to the concept of "praying through."
We can "pray through" until God lets us know we have victory in our prayer.
Likewise in praise and worship we can persist until we know we have the victory;
Heaven is opened and the enemy defeated.
In fact our persistence can create a continuous open Heaven.

Jacob wrestled with God until he was blessed:
So Jacob was left alone, and a man wrestled with him till daybreak.
When the man saw that he could not overpower him,
He touched the socket of Jacob's hip so that his hip was wrenched
As he wrestled with the man.
Then the man said, 'Let me go, for it is daybreak.'
But Jacob replied, 'I will not let you go unless you bless me.'
The man asked him, 'What is your name?'
'Jacob,' he answered.
Then the man said, 'Your name will no longer be Jacob, but Israel,
Because you have struggled with God and with men and have overcome.'
Jacob said, 'Please tell me your name.'
But he replied, "Why do you ask my name.'
Then he blessed him there.
So Jacob call the place Peniel, saying,
'It is because I saw God face to face, and yet my life was spared.(Genesis32:24-32)

Jacob knew he needed the blessing of God,
And he was not going to let go of God until he was blessed.
This needs to be the attitude of our worship.

The Season Of The Last Generation

WORSHIP GOD IN SPIRIT AND IN TRUTH

We must not let go of God until He manifests His Presence;
Until we see Him face to face; until we are blessed.

Praise Until The Spirit Of Worship Comes,
Worship Until The Glory Falls;
Then Experience Intimacy With Christ Jesus

This was the admonishment and attitude of Ruth Ward Heflin,
And came from her life long pursuit of God and her experience in God.
We can begin to praise God in the natural;
This enables us to get "in the Spirit."
Once we are "in the Spirit" we can worship Him until He releases His Glory,
His manifest Presence.
Then, we can enjoy intimacy with the love of our LIFE, Christ Jesus,
For as long as we desire.
This intimacy was the intoxication of The Day of Pentecost.
Once you have experienced this intimacy you will never be the same again;
You will know why David asked for "one thing" above all else.
One hour in this intimacy is worth a thousand hours
Experiencing what ever is second best.
You will never want to leave this intimacy; it is Heaven on earth.
For the rest of your life
You will desire this intimacy with Christ Jesus above all else;
Nothing else will satisfy you; you are spoiled for life,
Which is exactly what God wants to do for you.
The only thing standing in your way is your willingness to enter in.
Christ Jesus is waiting for you!

The Song Of Songs Teaches Us The Intimacy Of Worship

The following are paraphrases out of the Song of Songs put into poetic form;
It is The Bride of Christ speaking to her Lover, Christ Jesus
And Christ Jesus speaking to His Bride.

The Bride of Christ Speaking To Christ Jesus:
I belong to you my King
My desire is for you alone
Place me like a seal over your heart
Like a brand upon your arm
For my love for you is as strong as death
It burns like a blazing fire
An ocean of water cannot quench my love
A river cannot wash it away

All the wealth of this world
Is as nothing compared to our love.

The Season Of The Last Generation

Every delicacy both new and old
I have stored up for you my love
For my love for you is as strong as death
It burns like a blazing fire
An ocean of water cannot quench my love
A river cannot wash it away

Come away with me my lover my friend
Let me be your complete contentment

Let me be your complete contentment

Christ Jesus Speaking To His Bride:
Who is this that appears like the dawn
Fair as the moon Bright as the sun
Majestic as the stars all beautiful you are
There is no flaw in you

You have stolen my heart my sister my bride
With one glance of your eyes

How delightful is your love my darling
Better than wine, fragrant as perfume
You are a garden fountain, a well of flowing water
There is no one like you

You have stolen my heart my sister my bride
With one glance of your eyes

True Worship Creates Unity In The Body Of Christ
Unity In Worship Commands The Blessing Of God

True worship and praise to God creates "Oneness" with God as nothing else can,
And "Oneness with God creates unity in the Body of Christ.
In Heaven, all are ONE, and therefore they praise and worship the Living God.
On earth, when we worship in Spirit and in Truth, God makes us ONE,
By the power of His Spirit;
We are transformed by the words of our mouth, by Christ in us,
And He brings the unity in His Body He desires.
Unity in worship commands the blessing of God.
Behold how good and how pleasant it is for brethren to dwell together in unity!
It is like the precious ointment poured on the head, that ran down on the beard,
Even the beard of Aaron [the first high priest],
That came down upon the collar and skirts of his garments
[Consecrating the whole body]; [Exodus 30:25,30]

The Season Of The Last Generation

Like the dew of [lofty] Mount Hermon,
And the dew that comes on the Hills of Zion;
For there the Lord has commanded the blessing,
Even life forevermore [upon the high and lowly]. (Psalm 133, Amplified)

The Worship of Every Saint Matters And Makes a Difference

We are "living stones" built into The New Jerusalem, The City of God,
Who's architect and builder is God.
The worship of every saint adds to the whole, a living, necessary part,
And adds to the power of God released.
In worship every single saint makes a difference.
Every heart set on Christ makes a difference.
Every voice makes a difference.
Every pair of hands lifted up makes a difference.
Everyone dancing makes a difference.
Every act of worship makes a difference.
There are no insignificant acts of worship before the Living God.

The Remnant Who Turns Back The Battle At The Gate

In The Time of The END, The Bride of Christ will turn back the battle at the gate.

In that day the Lord Almighty
Will be a glorious crown, a beautiful wreath
For the remnant of His people.
He will be a Spirit of justice to Him (Christ) *who sits in judgment,*
A source of strength to those who turn back the battle at the gate. (Isaiah 28:5-6)

We have learned that the battle belongs to the Lord,
But we are His instruments of battle
As we enthrone Him in our praise and worship.
Lord make us instruments for Your Glory!

A Glimpse Of Heaven Inspired Praise

Praise the Lord
Praise God in his sanctuary;
Praise him for his acts of power;
Praise him for his surpassing greatness.
Praise him with the sounding trumpet,
Praise him with the harp and lyre,
Praise him with tambourine and dancing,
Praise him with the strings and flute,
Praise him with resounding cymbals.
Let everything that has breath praise the lord
Praise the Lord. (Psalm 150)

The Psalms Are Our Teacher
Many of the Psalms were born out of the Tabernacle of David;
Out of Zion, The City of God, where the fire of God resides.
The Psalms are our teacher.
They teach us the nature and character of Heavenly praise and worship;
Praise and worship that brings the Kingdom of God to earth as in Heaven.

Your Kingdom Come, Your Will Be Done, On Earth As In Heaven
This is the heart cry of the Church of the Living God;
This is the object of their unquenchable zeal;
This is what happens when the people of God worship their God
In Spirit and in Truth.
This is what happened on that "Holy Hill," Zion, in The Tabernacle of David;
This is the foreshadow of The New Jerusalem.

Christ Jesus intends for us to live continuously in His Presence.
When we worship God in Spirit and in Truth
We can live continuously in His Presence and His manifest Glory.
Then there is continuous victory over our enemies;
Then the plan and purpose for our lives and His Church is made complete.
This is where Christ Jesus is leading us at this time.
He is going to bring about the answer to His own prayer (John 17)
And make us ONE with Himself.

Shake off the spirit of religion that is only empty form,

Abandon yourself to God and see what He will do through you;

Exceedingly and abundantly above what you can think of ask

By His power at work in you!

Christ in you the hope of glory!

Hallelujah!

The Devil Seeks Worship

The devil seeks those who will worship him in his spirit, deceived by his lie.
He seeks those who will worship him in his spirit,
And embrace his lie, which he puts forward as the truth, as an angel of light;
That each person can be like God, doing as they please, ignoring the God of Heaven.
It is also notable that he receives what he seeks;
In terms of numbers, exceedingly more than does the God of Heaven.
The people of this world give to the god of this world, whole heartedly
The worship and glory that he wants.
Virtually all that goes on in the current culture, ie.: television, movies, politics,
Social events, rock concerts, sporting events, etc., are testimonies to this fact.
The people of this world are abandon to their god,
And this abandonment leads to eternal death.
The glory of the god of this world,
Is the willingness of most of humanity to follow him to their eternal death.
The world controlled by the devil puts on a show, a pretense, like a movie prop;
When you look behind it it is empty, without substance, without life;
The devil is the puppeteer, pulling the stings of a world he has deceived;
A world lost and destined for hell.

True Worship Stops The Expansion of Hell

True worship mitigates, arrests and stops the enlargement of the mouth of hell,
And the eternal carnage that the worship of the devil brings,
Worship of the True and Living God in His Spirit and in His Truth,
Brings Him the Glory that is due to Him,
And brings His Presence that destroys the works of the enemy.
This worship brings about the God consciousness that causes men to turn to Him.
All other endeavors for God must begin here.
Abandonment to the God of Heaven leads to eternal LIFE.
God gains glory when individuals and His Church abandon themselves to Him.
This is the destiny of The Bride of Christ;
Her love for Christ Jesus is as strong as death,
And burns like a blazing fire; Forever!
He brought Her from death to LIFE and She will never forget that!

ABOUT THE AUTHOR

Tom Haeg is an architect, writer, song writer and musician
Who has been a student of the Bible for more than 25 years.
He and his wife Susan have been blessed
To experience the outpouring of God's Spirit called "Renewal"
And have witnessed the manifest presence of God.
Tom and Susan's lives have been changed forever
By this encounter with the Living God;
Changed by His grace, love and power.

They have led worship in small groups and larger services
Where God has poured out His Spirit in marvelous ways.
Through this outpouring they have seen God change lives.

Tom has read extensively about the history of the Christian Church
And the revivals that God has visited upon His people
Up to and including this present time.
He believes that the Final Revival lies dead ahead,
Where God is going to pour out His Spirit in a magnitude
That has never been seen before.
Tom believes that this outpouring will precede the Great Tribulation
Spoken of in the Book of Revelation.
He believes that soon there will be thousands upon thousands of Christians
Ministering Christ Jesus in the power and fullness of Christ.
The name of Jesus will be upon every heart, mind and mouth
Every man woman and child
In every nation on the face of the earth.

Christ Jesus will present Himself personally to every living person on earth.
Every person will be given the opportunity to accept Him
As their Savior, Lord and Anointing.

Tom's other books include: "Called By Christ To Be ONE" and "The Time Of The END."

CPSIA information can be obtained at www.ICGtesting.com
Printed in the USA
BVOW06s1412190914

367581BV00004B/29/P

9 781451 553543